MW00883674

Enchanted Cottage

LINDA BLESER

DEDICATION

To my family for their unwavering support.

PROLOGUE

It was a beautiful day to die. Birds chirped with innocent abandon, and sunshine streamed through the beveled windows of the cottage. Somewhere music played soft and low.

A tear trembled at the corner of Elise's eye, trailing from her cheek to the pillow. It wasn't supposed to end like this. Their time together had been so short. Where was her happily ever after?

Elise took a deep breath and drifted, slipping away by degrees. Each time she woke it was harder to open her eyes. Her voice was no more than a whisper. "Robert?"

His hand closed around hers. "I'm here, sweetheart."

There was so much she needed to say but time was slipping away. She wanted to tell him to be happy without her, to love again and bring joy back to their enchanted cottage.

Robert's eyes, which normally sparkled like the sea, now drowned in tides of sorrow. She couldn't bear the thought of her husband being alone. *Be happy*, she wanted to say. *Find love again and bring joy to this magical place where time stood still for us.* "Promise me?"

"Anything, my love."

"Our cottage." *Don't be lonely here. Fill it with love again.* "Promise..." The words eluded her, slipping from her grasp like woodsmoke. The covers felt heavy and damp—suffocating. She gripped the edges, as if she could hold onto life with sheer willpower.

"I promise, darling." He laid his head on the pillow beside her and wept. As her eyes fluttered, he noticed the color had faded to a soft, wilted blue, as if the sky itself had been drained from them. Her hand curled in a tiny seashell beside her cheek and sunlight shimmered her hair to gold. She looked like an angel. A sleeping angel.

A dying angel.

A sob caught in his throat. He couldn't imagine a single day without her, let alone an endless lifetime. The future stretched before him barren and cold.

He vowed never to break his word to her. Nothing in the cottage would change from this day forward. His life would be altered forever, but the cottage would remain unchanged, a shrine to his love.

* * *

When Elise opened her eyes again it was twilight. She tried to speak, but the effort drained her. Robert stirred. She stared into his face. The face she loved. So sad, so weary, so hopeless. If only she could erase the pain there. She wanted to bring the light back into his eyes, see the smile return to his face, give him back a reason to hope. She wanted to stroke the hair from his forehead, wipe the sheen of tears from his cheeks, but her hand was too heavy to lift.

"Elise?"

His image blurred. There was more she needed to

say, but she couldn't form the words. Time was running out. *Love again.* Her brow furrowed with the effort. "Love..."

He brushed her hair from her forehead. "I love you too, my darling. Forever and always."

She struggled to speak, but he cradled her, rocking her slowly and tenderly. "Shhh."

She let go, drifting peacefully, feeling her husband's lips on her forehead and remembering the love they'd shared here in their enchanted cottage. "Cottage," she murmured. *Be happy here, the way it was meant to be.*

"I promise, my love. I'll stay here in our cottage. I'll keep it exactly as it is today. Forever and always."

And love again? Promise to find happiness after I'm gone. "Love..."

"Shhh...I promise, love."

She was too tired to fight. A long, slow breath of a sigh escaped her parted lips and she closed her eyes for the final time.

CHAPTER ONE

"Do you have to go, Mom?"

Liz Riley smiled. For a moment her daughter had sounded ten years old again. But she wasn't. Marcie was a grown woman with a family of her own now. As hard as it was to tear herself away, Liz knew her daughter and son-in-law needed time to bond with the new baby more than they needed an extra set of hands around. It was time to go home.

They stood beside the car, neither one wanting to be the first to say goodbye. These past few weeks had been wonderful, helping Marcie adjust to motherhood and watching her new grandson grow more adorable each day. It seemed like only yesterday she'd held Marcie in her arms, taking for granted the intoxicating blend of baby and talcum. She'd been so happy then, surrounded by children and other young mothers, busy with little league, bake sales and family vacations. Those days were full, frantic, and even frustrating at times. But never boring. Never lonely.

"Mom, are you sure you'll be all right driving all the way back home? I don't know why you didn't just fly."

Liz smoothed her daughter's hair from her cheek, tucking it behind her ear. Of her three children, Marcie was the most like her. Looking into her youngest child's face was like looking back in time—the same honey gold hair and eyes her husband used to compare to the swirl of brandy against crystal.

"I made it out here all right, didn't I?"

"Yes, but—"

"No buts. I'll be just fine. I've always wanted to see the country," Liz explained. "And I don't have to be back to work until school opens in September." That wasn't it exactly, but Liz didn't think her daughter would understand the feelings which had begun to creep up on her as she approached her fiftieth birthday—the feeling that life was passing her by, that the future held a series of endings rather than beginnings.

Marcie's brow furrowed. "It's just so unlike you, Mom."

"Now you're starting to sound like your brother," Liz replied. Teddy had practically put his foot down, implying she was too old to attempt a cross-country trip. Hearing her son tell her she couldn't do it alone had been the deciding factor. She'd packed her bags and set off, arriving safe and sound in California despite everyone's fear for her safety and sanity. Now after three weeks of helping her daughter adjust to motherhood, it was time to go home and she planned to enjoy every moment of the leisurely return trip.

"You'll call me when you get home?"

Liz smiled, wondering when the balance of worry shifted from mother to child. "Yes, of course I'll call you. I plan on taking my time along the way, so I can't say exactly when. I have my cell phone with me, so you don't have to worry."

"Are you sure you can't stay another few weeks?"

Liz gave her daughter a hug. "That's sweet of you to ask, honey." Her voice was husky with emotion. "But you need time alone with your new baby and your husband. Enjoy every day. Every moment. It goes by so quickly. One day you turn around and they're grown and you wonder where the time went."

Tearing herself away, Liz gave her daughter a final goodbye and climbed into the car. "We'll see you back home for Christmas, right? Teddy's coming home and Jill's bringing the kids. We'll all be together."

She regretted the words the moment she spoke them. Marcie's face tightened and her gaze turned inward. Of course they wouldn't all be together. They hadn't been since Ted died five years ago. Marcie had been Daddy's little girl and the years hadn't dimmed the sharp pain of losing her father.

"I miss Daddy."

"I know, honey. So do I."

Marcie's frown deepened. "Mom, why don't you move out here to California near us? Escape those winters back east. I hate thinking of you all alone."

"I'm not alone," Liz assured her. "I have my job and my friends and I'm still young enough to have fun. I'll be fine. Honest."

* * *

Back on the road her claims were less convincing. Lately she'd been feeling lonely and unfulfilled. She enjoyed the company of friends and co-workers, but the truth was, sometimes she felt a deep-down loneliness for a man, for intimacy. She yearned to touch and be touched.

Liz loved her job as nurse for the small elementary school her own children had attended, and could measure her life by the faces of the children she'd bandaged and comforted through the years. When those faces looked back at her from graduation and wedding photos in the local newspaper, she wondered where the time had gone. She'd settled into widowhood without a fight, forgetting that these were the years she and Ted had planned to travel and enjoy each other once the kids were grown and on their own.

Instead she began and ended each day in the same place, with no surprises in between. That's why this trip had appealed to her. Without adventure, her life would continue to slip away until one day she was too old to do anything but stare at yellowed photographs and regret the things she hadn't done.

Her itinerary would take her through eleven states from California to New York. She planned to take her time and veer from the route as the whim took her, exploring sleepy little towns, eating at out-of-the-way restaurants, and hitting every antique store and flea market along the way. Since she'd given herself permission to welcome the unexpected on this trip, there was no rush, no schedule to keep.

The first few days of her cross-country trip were uneventful. On the third, she found herself in the small, Victorian town of Coldwater Springs, nestled deep in the Colorado Rocky Mountains. Deciding that this would be a wonderful place to spend a few days sight-seeing, she checked into Stone Haven, a charming, historic bed and breakfast, for the night.

Despite her children's dire warnings, Liz was glad she'd made this trip. She felt exhilarated and more alive than she'd felt in ages, closer to twenty-five than the approaching fifty. She'd shed years on this trip, years which had dragged her down mentally as well as physically. It wasn't until she prepared for bed in the quaint inn that she remembered how far away twenty-five really was.

Studying herself critically in the mirror, Liz noted each minute sign of aging—from the tiny frown lines in her forehead to the slight sagging of her breasts. Silver strands flickered through her hair and a fan of delicate lines radiated from the corners of her eyes, but it was her hands where the change was most evident. The skin there was dryer, and an age spot shaped like a lopsided heart had formed on her left wrist.

Her sense of adventure deflated, and with it the illusion of youth. Every single one of those years seemed to stare back at her from the mirror. With a weary sigh, Liz slumped onto the edge of the bed. *Who was she kidding?* There was no way to reclaim those lost years.

"Oh, knock it off," she chided herself, shaking off the dark cloud before it grew into a full-blown depression. Maybe fifty sounded a thousand times older than forty-nine, but it wasn't as if she had one foot in the grave. Fifty was still young. So what if things sagged a little? She wasn't dead yet. It was time to put away the widow's weeds and let some fun and adventure back into her life.

It was with that single purpose in mind that Liz deviated even further from her planned route the next morning.

* * *

Robert walked faster, hoping to beat the storm. When he'd left his Jeep in the village for a tune-up, Herb Hepplewhite had offered him a ride home, but he'd preferred to walk the few miles back to his cottage.

He could smell rain in the air. Leaves curled upward, pale underbellies curved as if to cup the anticipated moisture. Swift dark clouds deepened the shadowed coolness of the woods around him, woods of overlaying colors from golden aspen to blue spruce, and every shade of green in between.

He never grew tired of exploring the beauty of the land around him. The soft rushing song of a mountain spring which fed into the river below welcomed him home. Turning onto the cottage path, the first drops of rain sprinkled through the canopy of leaves overhead. It didn't matter, he was home now.

As always, the first sight of the cottage in the distance brought a smile to his face. He could feel the magic of the cottage reaching out to him, welcoming him home. This was where he belonged, here at his cottage in the woods where Elise's memory lived on.

Tucked into the mountainside, the cottage blended into the scenery. He'd built it with his own hands as a wedding gift to his wife, fitting together bedrock gathered from the riverbank into arches and coves and nooks. He stepped inside, feeling the cottage enfold him, calm him, comfort him. He loved it as much as Elise had. It was home, and home tonight meant a fire, a solitary meal washed down with strong coffee, and a good book to fill the hours before sleep.

Just like every other night since he'd begun his life alone.

* * *

Liz had detoured from her route to stop at a local

antique store. It had been worth it. She'd spent the afternoon wandering a maze of rooms in a renovated Victorian structure, admiring an impressive array of furniture, pictures and memorabilia from the past. There she'd found a delicate cameo brooch and left with directions to a flea market a few miles farther along the winding, single-lane mountain road.

She spiraled along the mountainside, twisting and turning and winding higher as she admired the breath-taking view of the majestic Rockies. One turn of the road and the sky opened up to panoramic vistas of snow-capped mountains, and the next moment the world dipped away to valleys and foothills where the sky kissed the Colorado River below.

She lost track of time, and it wasn't until the sky began to darken and the first tentative drops of rain splattered the windshield that she decided to retrace her steps and return to the bed and breakfast for another night. She was sure she knew the way back, but each turn of the road only took her deeper and deeper into the mountains.

The rain pounded a torrent of fat drops against the windshield and the sky deepened to inky blackness. Her wheels spun on treacherous dirt roads turned to muddy, streaming ruts. Liz spotted lights in the distance, but rain and fog blurred her vision. As she squinted to make out the glow of lights ahead, the car began to slide. Just as she corrected the skid, her headlights flickered over something furry scrambling across the road. It was too big to be a cat, but smaller than a dog. She veered sharply, as startled eyes blinked from behind a raccoon mask.

Liz panicked when the rear wheels slipped in the

mud. She spun the steering wheel, frantically trying to bring the car under control, but it slid toward a ditch beside the road. Her heart pounded and her fingers gripped the wheel. The car slid and pitched sideways into the ditch, dipping and jerking to a stop against a tree trunk. The seat belt yanked her shoulder back as her head snapped sideways, glancing off the side window. She sat there for a moment, dizzy and trying to catch her breath.

"Damn it!" she muttered, shifting into reverse and feathering the gas pedal. The car only sank deeper, wheels spinning vainly in the mud. Out of sheer frustration, Liz gunned the engine over and over until it spluttered and died. She turned the key in the ignition and heard a dull click, but the engine refused to turn over. When repeated attempts failed, she sank back into the seat with a disgusted sigh, realizing the battery was dead. *Now what?*

Then she remembered the cell phone. All she had to do was call AAA and they'd have a tow truck here in no time—assuming they could figure out where *here* was. Liz rummaged through her purse and pulled out her phone. There was no signal. After several fruitless tries, she realized there probably wasn't a satellite transmitter this far in the mountains.

So much for having all her bases covered.

Up ahead, lights winked between the wind-lashed trees. It wasn't Stone Haven, but there was something in the distance. Liz swiped at the foggy windshield, focusing on the lights. It was a house, and it seemed to be the only one in sight. Rain drummed on the hood, ticking away the time as she tried to decide what to do next.

There were only two choices. Either she could knock on the door and ask to use the phone, or stay right where she was and hope to flag down another car on the road. Except there hadn't been any other traffic all afternoon, and another car might come around that curve and end up in the same ditch.

Deciding to take her chances with the house up the road, Liz took a deep breath and stepped out into the rain.

CHAPTER TWO

After the rustic log cabins, hunting lodges and dude ranches she'd passed along the way, the cottage seemed out of place, as if lifted from the pages of a fairy tale. Beveled windows glowed with a cheery welcome. Grateful to get out of the storm, Liz stepped into a stone alcove framing the doorway. Her first tentative knock on the door went unanswered. The wet chill of the rain numbed her fingers, making the flickering warmth beyond the windows even more inviting. She pounded harder.

When the door finally opened, the imposing silhouette that filled the doorway only added to the evening's chill. He stared at her, his face masked in shadows, waiting for an explanation.

Liz shook rainwater from her hair. "I had an accident down the road," she explained, pointing back into the darkness. "My car's stuck and I was hoping I could use your phone."

"No," he said abruptly, his voice as cold as the night.

Liz took a step back. She was tempted to turn and walk away right then and there, but a warm fire inside and the smell of coffee beckoned her. Besides, she hadn't seen any other houses nearby. He was her only hope. Obviously he didn't want her inside, but he could still help her. After all, small towns were known for their hospitality. *Didn't he know that?*

"Maybe you could call a garage for me, then?" she suggested. "I'll wait here...or in the car."

He cleared his throat, softening the bluntness of his reply. "Sorry," he muttered. "I meant the phone lines are down. You can't call anywhere."

Liz nodded, excusing his brusque response. Perhaps he wasn't as rude as she'd originally assumed.

"The power is out too," he said with a dismissive shrug.

She noticed candles flickering inside the room behind him. No power, he'd said. No phones. Yet there was warmth and light inside. She waited, not saying anything. Surely he wouldn't leave her standing out in the rain?

It seemed he would do just that. The seconds stretched to minutes. As her eyes adjusted to the dim light she made out his shadowed features. His eyes were cold and hard and his whole face crimped into a tight frown. Liz thought if anything she should be the one concerned with seeking shelter on a stranger's doorstep. Instead, he was the one reluctant to let her cross the threshold.

She cleared her throat, which broke through his frozen trance. He stepped aside slowly as if suddenly remembering his manners. "Why don't you come in and wait out the storm," he said, seeming to drag each word from some hidden recess.

She squeezed past him, muttering a brisk thank you, then stopped. Stepping inside was like entering the sanctuary of a church. Maybe it was the quiet hush of the room and the still pools of candlelight, but she couldn't shake the feeling she'd just entered a sacred shrine.

He closed the door and she turned to get a better look

at him. He was younger than he'd first appeared. In the warm glow of the firelight he seemed less angry than guarded. Her initial impression had been right. He seemed more afraid of her than she was of him. It was as if her very presence posed some kind of threat.

He gave her a quick, nervous smile, which was gone faster than it appeared. But it was a smile all the same, and it transformed his face. In that brief moment she saw something so vulnerable it tugged at her heart. With a shock she realized that he was handsome—handsome in a way that went deeper than bone structure and coloring. It revealed itself in his posture, emanated from the depths of his eyes, and multiplied a hundredfold at the brief, transitory curve of his smile. Realizing she was staring, she turned and looked around the room.

The interior, lit only by candlelight and a crackling fire, glowed with a fairy-tale charm. Homespun tapestries covered the walls and crocheted doilies draped over the arms of chairs and polished tables. Plump, overstuffed pillows in pastel shades and colorful braided rag rugs all spoke of a woman's touch.

As her gaze took in the surroundings, her senses picked up something else. There was an intense aura within these walls which both compelled and intrigued her, as if it could swallow her whole. The air seemed charged with a powerful, unnatural force. She could feel it pressing against her skin, making it tingle with excitement, swirling through her mind and bringing with it hazy impressions that felt like memories or visions. The air felt magical, dense with anticipation, as if she stood on the brink of some great discovery.

The strains of *Stardust* came from a portable radio perched on the stone fireplace mantle. The familiar melody triggered long-lost memories, transporting her back to a time when dreams were within reach and the future ripe with possibilities. An intense yearning for her lost youth gripped her and she closed her eyes, swaying to the music as she imagined strong arms around her, a whisper at her ear.

She moved beyond the threshold, humming to the music. When it stopped, she opened her eyes, remembering where she was. Again the cottage's owner seemed to have undergone a transformation. His gaze had softened and she realized the eyes that had looked so cold in the darkness were an intense blue. She was struck again by how young he looked when he relaxed the way he was now, leaning casually against the door frame. Late twenties, she guessed—about her son's age.

That didn't stop her from noticing the aura of sexual magnetism surrounding him. He was so handsome he took her breath away.

"You were singing," he said. His voice was softer now, less guarded.

"Stardust," she replied.

Another smile curled the corners of his lips, this time lasting longer before flitting away. "That's my favorite song."

She nodded. "Mine too." She studied him, doubting that he was old enough to remember the tune. He returned her gaze, leaning casually against the door frame. The long, lean angles of his body and his relaxed posture made her realize he'd adjusted to finding a half-drowned woman on his doorstep in the middle of a thunderstorm.

"I just made a pot of coffee," he said. "Would you like a cup?"

When she nodded, he left the room, returning a few moments later with two steaming mugs. She took one and wrapped her fingers around it for warmth, letting the steam curl up to her face.

"I thought the power was out?" She stopped, the mug halfway to her lips. As soon as the words were out, she realized they sounded like an accusation.

He chuckled, obviously not offended by her question. "We lose power all the time out here," he explained. "Especially when a storm rolls in off the mountains. I keep plenty of candles handy and I have a portable gas grill for emergencies. The coffee had just stopped perking when you knocked."

He pointed to a chair beside the fire. "Why don't you sit down and get warm. There's not much you can do right now except wait."

Liz saw traces of that same hesitation cross his face. It made her feel as if she were invading his space, despite his offer. "How long do you think it will take for the phones to be fixed?" she asked, pulling the chair closer to the crackling flames. The warm fire and hot coffee helped chase away some of the chill.

"It's hard to say. It could be a few hours, or a few days." He took a chair across from her, stretching his legs out toward the fire. "Where were you headed?"

"Coldwater Springs," she said. "I got a little carried away sightseeing today and lost my way. I was hoping to spend another night there before heading back to the East Coast."

"Whereabouts back east?" he asked.

"New York. A little upstate town no one's ever heard of." She told him about her trip, surprised to find herself so at ease with this stranger. Yet he didn't feel like a stranger for some reason, and she trusted her instincts. They'd never failed her before and they told her now she had nothing to fear from this man. There was something comfortable about him—something vaguely familiar, despite his reserve. That casual fall of thick, glossy-black hair, the deep, sparkling blue eyes and teasing grin.

She realized she hadn't introduced herself and held out her hand. "My name is Elizabeth Riley, but everyone calls me Liz."

A flash of emotions crossed his face and she saw everything from surprise to grief flickering in his eyes. He closed them for a moment, as if to hide the brief flare of pain reflected there.

"Are you all right?" she asked.

"Your name," he explained, drawing a quivering breath. "I thought you said..." The rest of the sentence trailed off, then he quickly recovered and explained. "My wife's name was Elise. It just took me by surprise for a moment."

Then, as if reminded of his manners, he straightened his shoulders and held out his hand. "I'm Robert. Robert Shane" He smiled, and this time he seemed to have brought the emotions under control, as if he'd had years of practice burying them.

"I'm sorry," she said. She knew without asking that his wife had died. She recognized the same pain in his eyes which she saw reflected from her own mirror every morning. "You never really get over losing someone you love."

That explained the signs of a woman's touch in the cottage. It also explained his reserve, the smile that came and went like a mirage. "How long has it been?"

He released her hand and hesitated, as if her question

had opened old wounds never fully healed. "Sometimes it feels like yesterday. Sometimes it seems a lifetime ago."

"I know," she said softly. "I lost my husband five years ago."

He cleared his throat, as if uncomfortable with the exchange. "To answer your question, Coldwater Springs isn't far from here. I'd offer you a ride, but my Jeep's getting a much-needed overhaul and won't be out of the garage for another day or so. It's too far to walk in this storm." He smiled apologetically. "I'm afraid you're stuck here. At least until the phone lines are fixed."

She couldn't think of any alternatives. She could wait the storm out in her car, but it was much more comfortable here. Besides, he made the best coffee she'd tasted in years. She'd forgotten how rich coffee tasted when you took the time to perk it rather than run a hasty pot through the drip coffee machine. She slipped her shoes off and angled her bare feet toward the fire.

"Warm enough?" he asked.

She nodded, trying not to stare at the dimple flirting at the corners of his smile. Her heart gave a little skip and she had to remind herself she was old enough to be his mother. She started to stand, but a wave of dizziness caught her by surprise.

He reached out to steady her, easing her back into the chair. "Are you all right?"

She nodded. "I bumped my head when the car went off the road. It's nothing to worry about."

Before she could stop him, his fingers brushed through her hair, stroking gently as he probed the edges of the swelling. "Don't move," he said.

Suddenly that was the last thing she wanted to do. She slumped into the chair. It wasn't the bump on her head making her weak, but his touch, which awakened feelings in her she thought she'd forgotten.

Robert came back with a first-aid kit. After cleaning the abrasion with a stinging antiseptic, he handed her an ice pack. "This'll keep the swelling down."

She tried to make light of it, denying the feelings his concern stirred within her. "Will I live?"

He smiled. "Yes, but you're not going anywhere tonight."

"But—"

"No buts. It's a three-mile walk through the back woods into town, nearly twice that far if you follow the road. In this weather, it's out of the question."

When she tried to argue, he put a finger to her lips. "Let's just take it a few hours at a time. If the power isn't back soon we'll discuss what to do from there, okay?"

Liz nodded. What choice did she have? It could be hours before they could call for help. She glanced at her watch and her heart gave a painful lurch. The watch hadn't survived the minor accident. The crystal was shattered, the hands frozen at the moment of impact.

Hot tears filled her eyes, blurring her vision. It wasn't an expensive watch, but it was the last gift Ted had given her the Christmas before he died. She'd worn it every day since, taking some comfort from keeping him close in a physical way. Seeing it broken and shattered felt like a final goodbye.

Carefully she slipped the watch off her wrist and swiped a tear from her eyes. It was only a watch—just metal and glass—but it reminded her that some things could never be fixed, no matter how much time you had.

Robert reached out and touched her trembling hand.

She smiled, but the corner of her mouth twitched as

she fought to keep from breaking down. She took a slow, deep breath and struggled for control. "My husband...my husband gave me this."

He nodded, understanding completely. For a long moment they were both quiet, then he stood, giving her shoulder a gentle pat before walking away.

Oh, now you've done it, Liz thought. First she'd invaded his space, an unwelcome intrusion he obviously resented. On top of that, now she'd gotten all emotional, making him even more uncomfortable. Draining the last of her coffee, she leaned back, taking slow, deep breaths until she felt some measure of calm return.

Liz heard Robert's soft footsteps and waited a beat before opening her eyes. When she did, she saw that he'd pulled his chair directly across the table from her. She watched him unfold a delicate, lace-edged handkerchief. With tender care he spread the handkerchief out on the table, his fingers lingering a moment on the embroidered "E" in the corner as he straightened the square of linen out.

Barely able to breathe, Liz watched Robert place her broken watch precisely in the center of his wife's handkerchief, a momento which must have been just as precious to him as the watch was to her. Then, with the same slow care, he brought the corners up, wrapping the shattered watch and then tucking it into an empty wooden matchbox. The way he handled it—so reverently— touched her in a way she hadn't been touched in years.

He handed her the box, holding it out carefully and closing her hand around it. She nodded with gratitude, unable to speak. Robert simply patted her hand and nodded back.

When she could finally speak around the lump in her

throat, she was desperate to lighten the mood. "I guess I'll have to depend on you to tell me what time it is."

He shrugged. "We—I mean, I—don't pay much attention to time here."

Liz looked around, suddenly realizing she hadn't seen a single clock in the room—not on the walls, mantle or end tables.

"Why...?"

Before she could finish the sentence, he cleared his throat and explained. "It was a small idiosyncrasy my wife had. Elise never allowed clocks or calendars in the cottage. Nothing to mark the passage of time. She imagined this cottage as the one spot on earth where time stood still, where the outside world couldn't intrude. It was a belief I found charming."

"And now?"

The smile wilted from his face, and his eyes, which had been focused on a faraway point in time, became guarded again. Just as quickly, the gruffness returned to his voice. "Now time is simply a painful reminder."

He looked around the room, as if searching for something to divert them both from painful memories. "Do you play Scrabble?" he asked, changing the subject.

His question was so out of the blue, it surprised a chuckle from her throat. "I love Scrabble," she admitted, welcoming the distraction. She'd been wondering how they would pass the time. "But I have to warn you, I'm a tough competitor."

"Well, I can't resist a challenge," he replied. "I believe you may have met your match."

He was right. The score flip-flopped back and forth. She admired his strategic use of the board and tiles. The portable radio played softly in the background, each song bringing her back to a sweeter time. She wondered if he kept it set to an oldies station. Some of those songs she hadn't heard in years.

He caught her daydreaming. "Everything all right?"

She smiled. "I'm just enjoying the music. They don't make music like this anymore."

"Music you can sway to," he agreed. "Would you like to dance?"

She almost said yes, then caught herself and blushed. Dance? Why would he want to dance with her? He was just being polite. "No," she said with a nervous laugh, avoiding his gaze. "I'm too dizzy, remember?" Before he could respond, she pointed to the board. "Look! I used all my tiles. That's an extra fifty points."

He tore his gaze from hers and stared at the board. "Glyptic? That's not a word."

"It is too! It means to engrave on gems."

"Who would want to ruin a perfectly good gem by engraving on it?" he asked. "Admit it. You made that up."

She tilted her head at him. "Are you challenging me?"

He seemed to consider it for a moment, his forehead creased in concentration. "No. I'll let this one go. Just don't make up any more words."

"Hey. I didn't make it up. Where's the dictionary? I'll prove it to you."

He sat back and crossed his arms over his chest, smiling. "Over there on the bookshelf." He tipped his head in the direction of the book case.

She felt his eyes on her as she crossed the room and a shiver went up her spine. *Get a grip,* she chided herself, reaching for the dictionary. Her gaze fell on a shelf lined with leather-bound volumes of fairy tales, everything from the Brothers Grimm and Hans Christian Anderson to the lesser known works of Giambattista Basile and Mme de Villeneuve. She trailed her fingers over the books.

His voice was wistful behind her. "My wife had a passion for fairy tales and folklore."

"I see that." Liz slipped a thin volume out and opened it, admiring an illustration of Sleeping Beauty, artfully arranged and peaceful in repose. She felt him come up behind her and held her breath, aware of him in a way she hadn't felt aware of a man in many years.

He reached over her shoulder, his fingers tracing the sleeping form. "Did you know that in the original version the King came across Sleeping Beauty in the forest, but instead of waking her with a kiss, he raped her and left her pregnant. When the Queen discovered his royal indiscretion, she ordered Beauty's twin children killed and cooked for the King's supper."

Liz shuddered.

"The children were saved," he continued. "The Queen was burned alive, and Sleeping Beauty and the King lived happily ever after." He shook his head. "Not a very nice message, is it?"

"I like the Disney version better."

Robert sighed, a far-away look on his face. "Elise preferred the romantic fairy tales to their earlier, more violent counterparts too. But then, Elise always believed in happy endings. Right up until..."

Liz felt something pass between them. An affinity so intense she had to remind herself to breathe. His arm curled around her shoulder with a gentle squeeze. Then he stepped away. She immediately missed his presence beside her. For a fleeting moment she was tempted to turn and step back into his arms.

Shaking the vision away, she returned the book to its place on the shelf. This wasn't a fairy tale, she reminded herself. But what was it about him that made her feel young and vibrant and alive? Why did she have to keep reminding herself of the years separating them?

When he spoke again, his voice seemed purposely formal and assuring. "It's getting late and the storm doesn't seem to be letting up. You're welcome to spend the night."

Liz was surprised to realize how much time had passed. Even while she shook her head, she realized there weren't any other options. Her hesitant refusal was more out of a sense of propriety than fear.

"I promise you'll be safe here until morning."

She knew that was true. She felt perfectly safe with him, safe within the warmth of his cottage. She refused to think about the fact that she'd checked out of the Bed and Breakfast without calling her daughter and no one in the whole world knew where she was. She could imagine her family's shock and disapproval. *You spent the night with a strange man in the middle of nowhere? What were you thinking?*

They'd have her committed.

Well, so what? "I'll get my things," she said, making up her mind and trusting her instincts. She was a big girl and could make her own decisions.

What about the attraction you're feeling, a small voice urged? She shook her head and reminded herself that she was twice his age and any fears of her reputation being compromised were groundless.

"No," he said, stopping her. "I don't want you going

back out into the rain. I've got everything you'll need right here."

Carrying a candle to light the way, he led her into a plush, feminine bedroom. The bed looked soft and inviting, with a down coverlet and embroidered pillowcases. A brass and crystal fluted reading lamp sat on the bedside table and a heart-shaped grapevine wreath sprinkled with tiny rosebuds and baby's breath was the only decoration on the wall above the brass headboard.

Robert spoke in hushed tones. "I stopped using this room after...well, I just felt more comfortable in the spare bedroom." He cleared his throat and showed her how to lock the door, as if anticipating her unspoken concerns. "I'm close enough if you need me, but you'll have complete privacy here."

He left the candle on the night stand and turned to the dresser. She watched him in the dusky shadows beyond the candle's glow. Above the dresser an ornate vanity mirror reflected the grief on his face when he opened a drawer and shook out a flowing white linen nightgown. He stood there for a moment, his shoulders tense, running his fingers over an antique vanity set on the lace runner.

She imagined he must be feeling overwhelmed by his late wife's presence in this room. She could almost feel him fighting the temptation to lift the brush and unwind a silken hair from the bristles. It tugged at her heart. She wanted to comfort him. She wanted to hold him and rock him and let him cry until there were no tears left.

He straightened his shoulders and turned, the nightgown draped over his arm. There was no sign on his face of the private grief she'd seen reflected in the mirror. She took the nightgown and thanked him. He moved toward the bed, as if to turn down the bed linen, then stopped.

"I'll do it," Liz said, reaching out for his arm.

He seemed relieved, smiling at her before moving toward the door. "Don't forget to lock up. I'll see you in the morning."

With a quick nod, she wished him goodnight. The room felt emptier after he left. For the first time she realized how isolated the cottage was, although she hadn't felt that way when Robert had stood beside her. Although she should have felt like an invader in this room, that wasn't the case. The room seemed to embrace her, as if welcoming her home. Strange that she should feel that way.

She blew out the candle, cracked the window half an inch, and watched lightning split the night sky. Now that she was safe inside, she could appreciate the storm's fury. In the darkness of the room she undressed and slipped the nightgown over her head. It smelled like sunshine and fresh air, as if it had been pulled off the clothesline just this morning. She took off her glasses and set them on the bedside table, then brushed her hair out, using the brush from her purse rather than the antique brush which had stood untouched on the dresser since its owner left. With a grateful sigh, she sank into the softness of the bed, realizing just how exhausted she really was.

Before sleep claimed her, the image of Sleeping Beauty came unbidden to her mind.

CHAPTER THREE

Unable to sleep, Robert stared out at the storm through rain-streaked windows. The night felt different. The house felt different. He could feel Liz's presence in the other room and he wasn't prepared for the sense of comfort that gave him.

His breath fogged the glass. He reached up and touched his finger to the spot once, twice, then traced an upward curve to form a happy face on the cool surface. Tears of condensation slid from the caricature's eyes. With an angry swipe of his fist he wiped away the crying happy face.

He tried to remember Elise's face, but the image blurred. He tried to capture her voice, but it was too far away, floating just beyond his reach. The fact that another woman slept in her bed filled him with guilt and confusion, as if he'd betrayed his wife's memory.

"Elise," he moaned, but his cry was lost in the rumble of thunder.

* * *

Liz tossed, twisting the covers into knots. She moaned, caught in a dream. There was a book, but the words made no sense. She tried to shape the letters into words, the words into sentences, and still the meaning eluded her. Frustration clenched her throat into a tight knot, and desperation made her tremble. She knew the words were important, but couldn't decipher them.

She twisted and turned, getting more tangled in both the sheets and the dream. Her throat tightened, forcing the words out with a strangled whimper. "Our cottage...our enchanted cottage."

A loud crash awakened her, jerking her from the dream. She sat up in bed, blinking and disoriented. It took a few moments to shake the cobwebs of sleep and remember where she was. Wisps of dream images swirled around her like smoke and she couldn't shake the feeling that there was something important she needed to remember.

She slipped out of bed and padded across the room. A flash of lightning startled her, illuminated her reflection in the mirror. For a moment it seemed she was looking into her daughter's face beyond the glass. The room went black again and she shook her head, blaming the vision on the darkness and the fact that she'd left her glasses behind on the nightstand. Putting the ghostly image out of her mind, she opened the bedroom door.

Robert stood silhouetted by the window. He turned when she entered the room and she joined him at the window, squinting into the darkness as flashes of lightning turned night to day. A crash of thunder followed, so loud that she jumped and gave an embarrassed laugh when he put his arm around her shoulder. Wind rattled the window pane and thunder rumbled off the mountains, vibrating through her entire body.

They stood side by side watching the storm rage outside. There was something comforting about viewing the storm from the safety of the cottage, something so reassuring about his arm draped protectively across her shoulder. She felt lost in time, lost in a world where there was no right or wrong. There was only the storm and this moment and the man beside her.

They stood there in silence staring out into the night for what seemed like an eternity. There was wildness to the pounding fury of the storm that made their silence even more intimate. Finally, her reservations overcoming her instincts, she pulled away. His arm dropped to his side and when another burst of lightning illuminated his face, he was staring intently at her. His eyes were dark and intense, as if seeing something more, something she herself couldn't see.

Maybe it was the nightgown. Maybe seeing her in it reminded him too vividly of his wife. She clutched her arms around herself protectively.

"Don't," he said. "You look lovely."

Something in his voice made her believe him. She hoped the darkness camouflaged the flush she felt rising to her cheeks before another flare of light could reveal her embarrassment.

You're acting like a schoolgirl, she chided herself. Yet that was exactly how she felt—young and virginal and blushing. And all he'd done was give her a reassuring squeeze on her shoulder, stare out into the night beside her, tell her she looked lovely. What was wrong with that?

I could be his mother, she scolded herself. *That's what was wrong with it.*

"Tell me about Elise," she said, hoping to fill the silence with something other than longing.

Lighting a candle, he moved to the sofa and settled

back, getting comfortable while he spoke. "We were so young and so in love. We built this cottage together and planned to spend the rest of our lives here."

The words that came from her lips were unplanned. She seemed to hear them for the first time. "Your enchanted cottage."

He jerked as if he'd been slapped, pinning her with a look from those flashing eyes. "That's what Elise always called it."

She nodded. Somehow she'd known that before he confirmed it.

In a voice as soft as the splatter of rain on the sill, he told her that Elise's dying words had been to ask him to take care of the cottage she so loved.

He looked at her, then away, but not before she caught the shimmer in his eyes. "I haven't changed a thing. It's exactly the way it was when she died. Exactly the way she left it."

She recognized the emotions that crossed his face. Loss. Grief. Emptiness. Without thinking, she joined him on the sofa, reaching out to squeeze his hand in hers. Silent tears slid down his cheeks and she drew him close, cradling his head on her shoulder as she stroked his hair. She rocked back and forth, comforting with the same hushed whispers and soft murmurs which had calmed her babies so many years ago.

She held him long into the night. Neither spoke, yet the silence was soothing, like a soft blanket wrapped around them. Eventually his breathing became deep and regular, and still she held him close until finally she too drifted to sleep, her chin resting against his forehead.

* * *

In the morning he was gone. She lay curled up on the couch, covered with a soft quilt. The memory of holding him in her arms was as hazy as the dreams which had led to her finding him alone in the dark last night.

Sunlight warmed her face. She jumped up, wrapping the quilt around her, and went to the window. The rain had stopped, leaving diamond droplets that glistened in the sun. She noticed things she hadn't seen in the darkness the night before. The cottage sat in the center of a glade alongside a crystal pond which must have been fed by one of many mountain springs that emptied into the river below. Wildflowers grew in abundance, framing the path beyond the door, with clusters of blue columbine nestled amid natural rock gardens.

She pushed open the window and took a deep breath of the clean mountain air, washed fresh by last night's downpour. What a beautiful place to live, she thought. The word *enchanted* came to mind and she frowned, wondering why it felt at once strange and familiar.

In the distance she saw Robert bending over the open hood of her car. When she flicked the light switch, nothing happened. The power was still out. She wondered how long it would take to fix it way out here in the middle of nowhere. There was no sound when she lifted the telephone receiver to her ear, not even the hum of static. It looked as if she'd be here a little longer.

She folded the quilt and carried it back to the bedroom. Folding it over the foot of the bed, she smoothed the wrinkles out carefully. Had Elise made this with her own hands? Had she lovingly formed each tiny stitch, dreaming of the warmth which would enfold them? Liz ran her fingertips along a row of delicate stitches, then froze.

Her hands.

She blinked and stared. Her hands were different. The skin was tight and pink and smooth, unmarred by yesterday's encroaching age spots. They were no longer the hands of her mother.

She swirled and caught her reflection in a gilt-edged cheval mirror. The woman staring back at her from the full-length reflection was someone else—someone she recognized from a lifetime ago. She remembered seeing the same reflection last night. At the time it had looked like her daughter's face, but Liz knew it was her own image—only younger. Last night she had chalked it up to darkness, but now morning sunlight streamed into the room.

She reached across to the night stand for her glasses and put them on, expecting to see the signs of age returning to her reflection. Instead of improving her vision, however, the glasses only blurred it more. She took her glasses off and put them on again. Amazingly, her vision was better without them. She didn't need the glasses anymore.

Her hands shook. The only explanation left was that she was still dreaming. It didn't feel like a dream, however. She crept closer to the mirror. There was no question about what she saw there. *She was young!*

"If I'm dreaming," she whispered, "I don't want to wake up."

She stood in front of the full-length mirror and twirled. Eyelet lace dipped and hugged the curves of her breasts, and folds of white linen draped and swirled around her ankles.

She was young again—beautiful and healthy and

glowing and gloriously young. Her hair fell in thick, luxurious waves to her shoulders, glimmering with golden highlights. Other than a cinnamon sprinkle of freckles, not a single wrinkle or blemish marred the smooth, blushing porcelain of her skin.

Finally, curiosity overwhelming her, she raised the hem of the nightgown and lifted it over her head. Her reflection took her breath away. Her body looked thirty years younger and at least fifteen pounds lighter, smooth and tight and glowing with health, poised at the brink of womanhood.

She couldn't remember ever looking so enticing. If she had at one time, she either hadn't realized or appreciated it before it was gone. Her breasts stood firm and high, capped with tawny nipples. Her waist sloped to softly rounded hips and the gentle curve of a tummy without stretch marks. She turned and admired her bottom, firm and silky soft above shapely legs. Whoever said youth was wasted on the young was right.

A sharp gasp drew her attention. She turned and saw Robert standing in the doorway.

"Beautiful," was all he said, but his voice held a husky resonance that carried more weight than his words.

When had he come in? She reached for the nightgown to cover her nakedness, then stopped herself. When was the last a man had looked at her that way? When was the last time anyone had called her beautiful without adding "for your age?" More importantly, when was the last time she'd believed it?

He took a step closer and she gave a slight nod of encouragement, unaware she was doing it until she felt her head bob. She whispered the word "please," not knowing whether it was *please-yes* or *please-no.*

Slowly Robert stepped into the room, unbuttoning his flannel shirt. She watched his fingers move along the material, transfixed like a rabbit caught in the rush of headlights, staring at the golden expanse of chest as he moved closer still, slowly taking off his shirt to reveal muscular arms and broad shoulders tapering to a slim waist. His jeans rode low on his hips, the waistband's button unfastened. Her gaze followed the wisp of hair trailing from his lower belly to the brass button of his jeans. Then further, following the invisible path over straining denim. She couldn't breathe.

He slipped the shirt off and reached out, draping it over her bare shoulders. A current of air rippled the delicate down of her arms as his hands hovered a heartbeat above her skin. The flannel caressed her, soft with age, warm with the memory of his flesh, fragrant with the combined aroma of cologne and man. His shirt embraced her, cradled her, enfolded her, and this intimate gesture left her feeling more vulnerable than when she'd stood naked in the morning sunlight.

When he straightened the collar at her neck, his fingertips grazed along the hollow of her throat, soft and feather-light. He pulled the shirt around her, fastening the button at her breast. The fabric dragged across her trembling skin, tormenting her nipples into awareness. She knew if he said a word, one single word, she'd surrender willingly.

His gaze never left hers—eyes so achingly blue, so intense and sincere. Every flicker of emotion was captured and emblazoned from their crystal depths. Her breath escaped in a long, trembling sigh.

When Robert worked his way downward, buttoning the shirt around her body, she felt the faintest whisper of contact above her clenched thighs, a rustling caress. It could have been the corner of the shirt. Or a breeze. Or it could have been, might have been…

She looked away, breaking eye contact, willing herself to gain control. A shiver rippled through her body and he drew the shirt tighter around her as if warding off a chill. But she wasn't cold. Not at all.

Tucking a finger beneath her chin, he tilted her head until she was looking at him and brushed his thumb gently across her lips. Back and forth, back and forth, until her lips throbbed with the need to be crushed beneath his.

She knew all she had to do was ask, but she couldn't find the words, couldn't find the strength to fight the accusations attacking her. *He's so young. What am I doing here? I don't even know him. I'm a grandmother, for God's sake!* Her mind and her body were at war and her mind was winning.

As if reading the hesitation in her face, he released her. "Maybe you'd better finish dressing," he said, holding her gaze for a moment longer before turning to stride from the room.

CHAPTER FOUR

Robert fought to control his emotions. The sight of her bathed in sunlight, the radiance of her skin, the way her eyes opened in wonder, then softened as they met his, nearly made him come undone. He tried to breathe, tried to quell the trembling of his hands where the sensory satin of her skin still lingered.

"Oh Lord, what have I done?"

When she emerged from the bedroom she still wore his shirt over her jeans from last night. Seeing her in his old plaid flannel tugged at his heart. She looked like a little girl in the oversized shirt—soft, innocent and vulnerable.

"I'm sorry," was all he could say.

She shook her head, excusing him with a quick smile. But he knew what he'd done was inexcusable. He should never have entered the room when he'd glimpsed her standing there. He should have simply walked away without letting her know he'd intruded on her privacy. He felt like a voyeur. And this, after assuring her she was safe in his home. He wondered if she'd trust him now, especially in light of what he was about to say.

He cleared his throat and looked away. "I'm afraid I have bad news."

"What's that," she asked.

"I checked your car. The battery is still dead and it's

hub deep in the ditch out there. We'll need a tow truck to get it out."

She frowned and he wondered what she was thinking. Did she fear this was all a ruse on his part to keep her trapped here? Was she afraid of him now? Afraid to spend another moment alone with him?

Her next question caught him off guard.

"Robert, what do you see when you look at me?"

He weighed his answer carefully, unsure whether she was referring to their earlier encounter and all too aware of just how much of her he *had* seen. He tried not to let the image of her dressed only in sunlight affect his reply.

"I see a woman with the most caring eyes and soul I've ever encountered. A woman willing to spend the night comforting a stranger. I see a woman who knows compassion, who has known and lost love and found the strength to carry on alone."

That wasn't what she'd expected. She measured his words to find the answer she was looking for. Was that all? Did he see her as young too?

"I see a beautiful woman," he continued. "In body and soul."

She read something else in his eyes. Desire. The same desire she'd felt in his arms. As much as she wanted to believe it was possible, she couldn't. "But Robert," she blurted out. "I'm older than you are."

She wasn't prepared for the warmth of his chuckle. "Are you?"

"Yes."

He led her to a mirror where their reflections stared back. His warm and inviting, her own solemn and dazed.

"What do *you* see?" he asked, holding her gaze in the mirror.

A hallucination of some sort, she wanted to say. A dream. A vision. A product of wishful thinking.

But whatever spell had been cast over her was still there. She looked young and innocent, a perfect match for the golden-skinned man standing behind her. He ran his hands up her arms, leaving a shiver where the fabric moved beneath his touch and caressed her skin.

When was the last time she had felt this way? When was the last time she had let passion ignite her body and bring a blush to her cheek? Was it wrong for her to want one brief, bright flare of those forgotten emotions?

She leaned her head against his shoulder. They looked so right together, her head barely grazing his shoulder. If she'd seen the two of them walking down the street together she would have sighed and smiled at the image of young love. What magic had brought her here? What magic held her captive? She didn't belong in his world, and he was too young to take back to her own.

He held her close, staring at her eyes in the mirror. Their images wavered and blurred together.

"What is age?" he asked. "Is it what you see in the mirror? Or is it the experience life has given you? Who's to say a person who packs a lifetime into a few years is younger than the person who hasn't lived at all?"

Her mind was spinning. She thought of her own children. Teddy, her oldest, was a perpetual boy who would never settle down, always seeking bigger adventures and thrills. Her middle child, Jill, was born mature beyond her years. Jill had always been older than Teddy, if not in years, at least in spirit.

"So," he said softly. "What is age? And does it matter?"

She wished with all her heart she could say no, it

didn't matter.

He turned her in his arms. She started to argue and he placed a finger over her lips.

"Don't think," he whispered. "Just feel. Feel how right this is. Feel with your heart."

She did, letting go of logic, letting the weight of doubt lift and free her to express the emotions struggling to the surface.

"Robert..." Her voice quivered, but his name felt right on her lips.

He brushed his finger across her lips, as if capturing her voice in his hands. "Say it again."

"Robert."

He leaned forward, slow enough to stop if she showed the slightest doubt. What she felt instead was a blossoming of desire that left no room for doubts. She welcomed his lips when they met—welcomed him with a passion that stunned her, made her weak, and dispelled any lingering doubts in her mind.

As they kissed she formed his name over and over against his lips. "Robert... Robert...Robert."

A wave of dizziness washed over her and he broke the kiss, his arms protective around her as he drew her away from the mirror and guided her to the couch.

"You're in no condition to drive yet," he said. "But now that the storm's over, I'll walk back to the garage in town."

She started to argue, but he stopped her. "I have to pick up my Jeep from the mechanic anyway, which I was planning to do today. I'll just send him back with the tow truck."

His thumb grazed across the backs of her knuckles, making it harder to think. As if realizing his effect on her, he released her hand. She felt the loss of his nearness so keenly she wanted to pull his hand back and never let go.

"But I still don't think you're up to driving," he said. "Not yet. Not until this dizziness passes." He smiled. "Until then, I'm afraid you're stuck here for a little while."

"And you're stuck with an uninvited house guest."

He frowned in mock consternation and twirled a lock of her hair around his finger. "Whatever shall we do?"

She blushed at the thought that immediately sprang to mind and tried to match his teasing banter. "I say we do breakfast."

"Hungry, are you?" His bantering tone seemed to imply that more than food was involved in the offer.

"Very." She tipped her head and stared at him, then lowered her gaze, looked away and back with a smile. *My God, he's flirting with me. And I'm flirting back! My kids would be horrified to see their mother acting this way.*

No sooner had the thought surfaced than she pushed it away defiantly. Whatever magic spell the cottage had spun, she wasn't ready to give up yet. Perhaps she didn't fully appreciate her youth the first time around, but this time she wanted to drink it in and treasure every moment. She wasn't ready to give it up just yet.

She followed him into the kitchen. While he lit the gas burners on the portable stove, she filled the percolator with water and coffee grounds scooped from a matched set of tin canisters.

She couldn't help noticing the feminine touches here in the kitchen, as well. Sheer, dotted Swiss curtains in sunny lemon framed the windows. Calico cushions softened the edges of oak dining room chairs. A potted

Philodendron draped glossy leaves over the top and sides of a glass-fronted hutch filled with neatly stacked rows of china and cut crystal.

It should have been eerie, as if the woman who'd cared for it so lovingly still wandered through this kitchen. Liz could almost see her pale ghost straightening the tablecloth, wiping a spill from the counter, restocking the pantry, humming as she prepared her husband's meal.

Yet she didn't feel like an intruder. The kitchen was warm and welcoming and the thought that came next nearly took her breath away.

I've come home.

She shook her head. What was she thinking? She was as far away from home as she could possibly be. Not only in space, but time as well.

Robert reached out to steady her. "Are you all right?"

"Yes, I just..."

"Why don't you sit down and let me take care of breakfast. I'm a whiz with pancake batter."

She did, letting him think it was the bump on her head making her dizzy rather than the swirl of emotions assaulting her senses.

Robert looked completely at ease in the kitchen. Soon the room was warm with aromas and the sounds of breakfast being prepared. Coffee bubbled lazily in the percolator and cinnamon sprinkled batter sizzled on the grill beside curling strips of bacon.

Liz touched the lump on her forehead, which had swelled to twice its size this morning. The thought struck her that perhaps she was hurt more seriously than she realized. Maybe she was at this moment lying in a hospital bed with a severe concussion. Everything else— the man cheerfully preparing and serving breakfast, along with the fountain of youth she'd discovered—were just by-products of a fevered brain and delirious dreams.

But if this was a dream, she never wanted to wake up.

"Penny for your thoughts," Robert said, carrying a steaming stack of pancakes to the table.

She took a deep breath of the breakfast spread before her and sighed. "I was just wondering when was the last time I was served breakfast by someone I didn't have to tip."

He offered her a cruet of pecan-flavored syrup and their fingers brushed, soft and tentative. A warm flush rose to her cheeks. She watched a pat of butter melt into a lazy pool on the stack of pancakes as time seemed to twist and turn and catch. A sense of *deja vu* overwhelmed her when she looked across the table and caught him watching her. The sense of having been here before intensified until there was no question of having been here before, but rather how often. *How many breakfasts had they shared? How many mornings had he raked her with a passionate gaze which fueled a hunger deeper than food could satisfy?*

Before she could analyze the feeling it was gone and whatever wrinkle in time had paralyzed her momentarily disappeared.

She realized he'd been talking and she hadn't heard a word he was saying. He gazed intently at her, as if waiting for an answer.

"I'm sorry," she said, trying to cover her distraction.

"You're free to explore all you want while I'm gone."

"Gone?" Her throat clenched, making her voice come out as a squeak. When he smiled it was as if he could read every one of her thoughts. But the smile did little to lessen the panic she felt.

"I won't be long," he said, grazing his fingertip along her wrist.

Then she remembered. He was going into town this afternoon to call a mechanic. Right on the heels of that thought was the realization that she didn't want him to go. She didn't want her car fixed, didn't want to have to decide whether to leave, even though she knew she couldn't stay.

CHAPTER FIVE

After Robert left, Liz decided to take him up on his offer to make herself at home. She desperately craved a long, relaxing bath and a fresh change of clothes. There was more to the desire than her own comfort, though. She wanted to primp and pretty herself and greet him at the door in a cloud of soft sweetness. All she needed were a few things from her car.

She stepped outside and lifted her face to the sunlight, taking a deep breath and filling her lungs with the crisp, clean mountain air. Her body thrummed with energy as she jogged to the car, feeling each blade of grass bend beneath her bare feet. *Had wildflowers ever smelled as sweet? Had colors ever been so brilliant? Had she ever felt so wildly alive?*

Giddy with excitement, her jog turned into a sprint, her sprint became a gallop, and her body responded with a burst of vitality she hadn't felt in years. She felt as if she could keep up this pace for hours without drawing a bead of sweat and chided herself for slacking off these past few years. Not just on her lack of exercising, but everything. She'd settled into a long, dull routine, allowing herself to feel old and tired and useless before her time. Used up. She'd forgotten how much pleasure there was in the simple enjoyment of her body's movements.

She stopped at the edge of the road, feeling her lungs expand with each breath. A bubble of pure joy escaped her throat in a surprisingly girlish giggle. She caught herself automatically looking both ways before crossing the road, despite the fact that she hadn't seen another car on the road since she'd been here.

Halfway across the dirt road, her shoulders began to slump. She felt winded and a sharp pain burrowed beneath her breastbone, making her pause to catch her breath. Suddenly the air felt heavier, sharp and rough in her lungs. Feeling as if she'd run a thousand miles, she staggered across the road and leaned against the car. The world tilted and spun around her.

Why was she suddenly so tired? Tired beyond exhaustion, as if she'd traveled through two decades in the last few moments. Maybe it was the bump on her head. She'd overdone it, that's all. Taking deep breaths and massaging the catch in her side, she regained her equilibrium. Slowly.

While trying to catch her breath, she inspected the damage to her car. The ditch she'd ended up in wasn't deep, but she'd definitely need to be towed out of it. Her front bumper was crumpled against the Douglas fir which had stopped her slide and jerked her forward against the steering wheel. Other than a broken headlight, she didn't see any other damage. With a little work she could be on her way in a day or so.

The thought brought a frown to her face. She wasn't ready to leave. Not yet.

She pulled the back door open and reached for her bag. It wasn't that heavy, but she had to strain and pull against gravity since the car was tilted away from her and soon found her breath coming in short, hard gasps as another wave of dizziness nearly brought her to her knees.

Setting her bag on the road beside her, she shut the car door and leaned her forehead against the cool window glass. After a few minutes her pounding heartbeat returned to normal and she straightened. She caught sight of her blurred reflection in the car window and automatically reached for her glasses, remembering too late that she'd left them behind on the nightstand.

But even without her glasses she knew what she was seeing. She was old again. Just when she'd started to believe she'd been magically transformed, it was torn away. She looked at her hands, seeing the delicate spiderwork of veins where only moments ago had been smooth, tight porcelain skin.

"Not yet," she whimpered. "I didn't even have a chance to enjoy being young again." One glorious sprint through the woods, a hint of flirtation, a moment of renewed invigoration. It wasn't fair. She hadn't fully explored the brief visitation of lost youth.

Robert! She couldn't let him see her this way. How long before he'd be back? She glanced at her useless car. There was no escaping. She had no choice but to go back and wait for him, then leave once her car was repaired. With a sigh, she carried her bag across the road. She might as well at least take the bath she'd been looking forward to. Skip the primping, the perfume and make-up. Forget about welcoming him home. At least she'd be presentable when she said goodbye.

With determination, she straightened her shoulders and headed back, her step becoming more brisk and firm as she moved toward the cottage. The closer she came, the more strength she felt returning to her body. She knew without even checking that the transformation had somehow reversed itself again

She stopped as a sudden realization gripped her. Hadn't Robert said that time stood still within the cottage walls. He'd even pointed out that there were no clocks or calendars. Nothing to mark the passage of time. The thought was persistent, no matter how much she tried to defy it with logic.

It was the cottage. The *enchanted* cottage. That was the source of the magic, her fountain of youth. As soon as the thought came, it rooted and took hold. The logic slipped into place with the ease of an unquestionable, undeniable truth. She didn't know why. She didn't care how. She just knew it was true.

Trembling, she lifted her hand to the sunlight. Turned it, studied it. The faded age spots were gone, the tracery of blue veins had disappeared. Her knuckles were smooth, her skin firm. That was all the proof she needed.

She unzipped the side pocket of her bag and dug for a hand mirror, confirming what she already knew. As further proof, she walked back to the road, realizing she must be reaching the limits of the property, the extent of the cottage's magical field. She held up the mirror, watching the passage of time in her reflection as she reached the road until her face once again became that of a woman on the brink of her fiftieth birthday.

Then she reversed her path, moving back toward the cottage and turning back time with each step. Could it be that simple? Or was she still hallucinating?

With a shock, she realized that she'd already been at the cottage's threshold when Robert had first set eyes on her. He'd never seen her as she really was. To him she'd always been young and beautiful. No wonder he'd laughed when she'd argued that she was older than he was. He couldn't see any discernible difference in their ages. They were both young and alive and full of passion. Inside the cottage her body was unchanged. Within the cottage's boundaries she could be young again.

Lifting her luggage with ease, she raced back to the cottage and the bath that awaited her. She still had an hour. Maybe more. Maybe much more.

* * *

Herb Hepplewhite grabbed two ice-cold colas from the cooler and handed one to Robert.

"Get much damage up there from the storm?"

Robert leaned back on the metal chair and lifted his legs onto the wooden milk crate which served as both table and foot rest in the garage. "Other than the power and phones being down, no."

"And the road being washed out," Herb added.

"Yeah, that too," Robert agreed.

Herb wiped his hands on his greasy overalls. "Well, your Jeep's ready once the road's clear. I changed the oil and gave her new plugs and points. The brakes look good. Of course, you don't give the old gal much of a workout."

"I'm not worried about the Jeep," Robert said. "I was hoping you could get the tow truck up there. Last night in the storm, a woman went off the road and into a ditch. Luckily she wasn't far from the cottage and could come in out of the rain. But with the phones down..."

Herb raised a grizzly eyebrow at his long-time friend. "A woman? And she spent the night?"

Robert chuckled. "Get your mind out of the gutter,

you old dog you."

Herb shrugged. "Hey, all I'm saying is that you don't let anyone inside that place of yours. Even your best friend. I haven't been inside the cottage since Elise died."

At the sound of his late wife's name, Robert grew quiet. Herb was right about two things. Despite the distance he kept from others, Herb was the closest thing to a best friend he had. And yes, Robert didn't allow anyone within the sanctity of the cottage. Not since Elise's death. Maybe it was his way of holding onto the past by not allowing the present to intrude. But there were other reasons, too. Things even Herb wouldn't understand.

For a long time he'd been practically a hermit there. Even on those rare occasions when he left his mountain haven, he left his heart behind. Herb hadn't let him lose himself in grief, however. He'd called and hounded him, finally convincing Robert to come over for a game of chess, which had, over the years, turned into a weekly event. At first Robert had fought the intrusion on his pain, but little by little Herb had coaxed him out of seclusion. At least physically.

Herb cleared his throat, clamping a work-roughened hand on Robert's shoulder. "I'm sorry."

Robert smiled at this friend, knowing he meant well.

"It's not that," he said, his brow furrowed. "It's this woman I told you about. There's something about her that reminds me of Elise—a regal beauty I've only seen once before." He stopped, knowing there was no way to explain it. He tried to put his finger on it. Her eyes were different, the shade of her hair, the curve of her lips. But sometimes she'd tilt her head a certain way, or an emotion would cross her face which made him catch his breath.

A bittersweet smile curved his lips and he shrugged his shoulders. "She touches me. She touches me in a way I thought I'd never be touched again."

The gentle hand tightened at his shoulder. "Maybe that means it's time to let go, my friend."

Let go? No, he could never let go completely. Maybe he could loosen his grip just a little, however. Enough to allow room for someone else in his life without breaking his vows or his promise to his Elise.

He straightened and both men looked away, as if uncomfortable with their emotional brush. "So," Robert said. "Guess I'll head back now."

"Want a ride as far as the bridge?"

"Nah, I like the exercise. Besides, it's quicker through the woods."

Herb held out his hand. "Better you than me," then coughed and asked, "What's her name?"

Robert didn't have to ask who he was referring to. "Elizabeth...Liz."

Herb nodded, as if that explained everything.

Before Robert got as far as the door, Herb's wife Janie bustled in, carrying an overflowing platter of chocolate chip cookies swaddled in plastic wrap.

"You're not leaving without cookies," she said.

Robert chuckled and took the platter from her hands. The plate was warm, proof that the cookies were fresh out of the oven. "Of course not," he said, bending to kiss Janie on the cheek.

"Did I hear—"

Herb cleared his throat loudly, interrupting his wife's chatter. Robert guessed that behind him, Herb was probably shaking his head and drawing a finger across his throat in an exaggerated "cut" motion to his wife. Not that he'd ever known anything to stop Janie if she smelled gossip.

Janie pursed her lips, seeming to give her husband's warning due consideration. Grudgingly she nodded and patted Robert's arm. "We'll talk later."

"I'm sure we will," he said with a chuckle, taking his leave before Janie changed her mind.

As Robert strode away, Herb draped his arm over Janie's shoulder. "What do you think, Janie?"

She shook her head. "I can't believe he's actually let someone into the cottage. He never lets anyone up there."

Herb pursed his lips and harrumphed. "Not even his best friend."

* * *

While the tub filled, Liz unpacked a fresh change of clothes, her terry-cloth bathrobe, and cosmetic bag. She would have boiled water for a bath if she'd had to, but luckily that wasn't necessary. When they'd washed the breakfast dishes, Robert had explained that the gas-powered hot water heater ensured they'd have plenty of hot water, even without electricity. Grateful for small favors, she sank neck-deep into the old claw-footed tub.

The warm water and bubbles worked their soothing magic into her muscles, calming her nerves and easing her worries. Suddenly it didn't matter whether things made sense or not. Logic fled as she closed her eyes and imagined a life of contentment right here in this timeless paradise.

Her skin tingled, a tingle that went deep inside, finding nooks and crannies nearly withered with neglect, tentative emotions surfacing from shadowed caverns. She lifted a handful of bubbles and blew, scattering them to float in iridescent clouds. She didn't want to leave. She wanted to stay here forever and explore the lost options laid out before her, to taste old emotions in new ways.

She wanted life. She wanted love. She wanted Robert.

Her mind drifted as she spun out a fantasy world where she was forever young and desirable. A world where wildflowers blossomed in riotous colors, where the air was fresh and the water crystal clear.

If only the choice were that easy. She couldn't just disappear. *What about her kids? Her job? Her friends?* With a sigh she stepped out of the tub and pulled the stopper, watching the water, like her fanciful dreams, swirl away. She towel dried her hair and let it curl naturally while she sat on the curved edge of the ceramic tub and pampered her body with almond-scented lotion that left her skin satin smooth, followed by a spritz of vanilla cologne at each pulse point.

She had one arm in her bath robe when a sound from outside the bathroom made her stop and hold her breath. It was a stealthy sound, as if someone were sneaking around out there. She tugged the robe tight around her, tying the sash and feeling safer somehow, as if the soft terrycloth was a suit of armor. She'd locked the door rather than risk a repeat of this morning's embarrassing episode. But still...

"Robert?" she called, her voice barely above a whisper. "Robert? Is that you?"

No answer.

Now she regretted calling out as the sounds beyond the door stopped. If someone had broken in, they knew she was here.

Another sound, this time a scrabbling, scratching sound, convinced her it was an animal, a fact confirmed when it emitted a sound somewhere between a mewl and a hiss.

Rats? God, she hated rats!

But she wasn't thrilled about being trapped in the bathroom either. She'd hoped to be dressed before Robert got back. Meeting him in various stages of nakedness was starting to become a habit with her.

Her desire to avoid another embarrassing incident overcame her fear of possible rats outside the door. She hadn't heard a sound in the last few minutes. Maybe she'd scared them away. She looked around the small room for something to arm herself with. The closest she could find was a toilet bowl brush, which wasn't much of a weapon, but did make her feel a bit braver. At least now she was armed.

She opened the door a crack and peeked out. There was no sign of anyone or anything from what she could see. She opened the door further, getting a better view. Nothing. Holding the brush in front of her, she stepped cautiously through the doorway, her gaze scouring the room for any signs of movement.

Seeing no signs of an intruder, she relaxed, realizing how silly she looked brandishing a toilet bowl brush. *Thank God Robert hadn't come back and seen her like this!*

She leaned against the couch, feeling foolish when something soft and furry brushed against her ankle. A flash of brown and black scurried past her. She jumped, a high squeal escaping from her throat. The animal turned back, giving her an outraged glare from its black masked eyes before escaping through the kitchen doorway.

Oh jeez wild animals! It was hard to tell who was more frightened—her or the baby raccoon she'd surprised. Now she really felt silly, but she'd be damned if she was going to run through the cottage in her housecoat trying to flush out a possibly rabid animal with a toilet bowl brush.

Straightening her shoulders, she marched into the room she already thought of as *hers* and locked the door behind her.

CHAPTER SIX

As always, walking through the back woods helped clear Robert's mind. There was something about the fresh air and exercise that swept the cobwebs away and put things in perspective.

The truth was, he'd been alone too long and had been momentarily tempted by the pleasure of another person's company. Having a woman in the house reminded him of things he'd buried inside, feelings that hurt too much to remember. As much as he enjoyed her company, Robert knew that Liz didn't belong here. Fate may have thrown them together for a brief moment, but time and space would keep them apart. She had a life to return to, and he could never leave the cottage.

Yet he couldn't deny the feelings she stirred in him. "Feelings I thought were dead," he murmured. "Feelings that—"

A shrill cry of alarm coming from the direction of the cottage brought him to a halt. He cocked his head and listened, but there was no other sound, just the echo of that one brief scream. He knew it was Liz, and the knowledge sent him running, crushing the plate of cookies against his chest and picking up speed as he neared the cottage.

He threw open the door and called out. "Liz? Liz, are you all right?"

Her muffled voice came from behind the closed bedroom door. "I'm fine. Give me a minute, I'll be right out."

Thank God, she was all right! Setting the plate of cookies on the table, he took a deep breath as his pounding heartbeat returned to normal. Only now that he was sure she was safe could he admit how worried he'd been.

But why had she screamed?

A scrabbling sound from the kitchen seemed to hold the key to that question. He went in and saw the raccoon sitting on the windowsill.

"Tallulah, did you scare the nice lady?"

The little raccoon sat up and wrung her paws, staring at him with intelligent eyes behind a black bandit mask, as if insulted that he would think such a thing. He scooped her up and she nestled in his arms like a tiny teddy bear.

He carried the raccoon back into the living room just as Liz was emerging.

"Robert, I hate to tell you this, but you've got wild..." Her voice faded as she saw the baby raccoon snuggled in his arms.

"I'm sorry," he said. "I should have warned you about the babies. They think they own the place."

"Babies?"

He chuckled at her shocked expression, but couldn't take his eyes off the rest of her. She looked so soft and touchable in a delicate pink sweater and leggings. Damp tendrils of hair clung to her neck and there was a fresh-scrubbed glow to her cheeks. He had to fight the urge to scoop her up in his arms and keep her safe and protected...and loved.

As quickly as the thought came, he pushed it away. How could he betray Elise's memory like that?

"The baby raccoons," he said. "This is Tallulah, so named because she's quite the little actress. Her favorite treat is chocolate—with almonds. I'm sure that's what she was searching for when you frightened her."

"*I* frightened *her*?"

Robert placed the ring-tailed bundle of fur on the couch and went to the cabinet, coming back with a foil-wrapped chocolate bar. He handed the raccoon a square, which she held daintily and nibbled on while she kept a wary eye on Liz.

"Their mother was hit by a car when they were just newborns," Robert explained. "Their eyes weren't even opened yet. I had to coax them to eat through an eyedropper with a mixture of canned milk and karo syrup. Finally they were old enough to be weaned to baby food, then dog kibble and table scraps."

He handed Liz a square of chocolate. She held it out to the raccoon, who hesitated, looking from her to Robert and back before greed overcame distrust. She wobbled over to Liz and took the chocolate, then returned to Robert's side before eating it.

"They're old enough to hunt and return to the wild, but they still come back to visit and beg treats from me."

"You say there are more of them?"

"Two brothers—Rhett because of his I-don't-give-a-damn attitude, and Rocky, who's the clown of the litter. You're lucky it wasn't Rocky who found you here. He'd have had your bags packed and your car running before I got home."

"She really is cute." As if suddenly finding her manners, Tallulah shuffled over and sat up in front of

Liz, who handed her another square of chocolate to seal their friendship.

"Speaking of your car," Robert said, watching the interaction with amusement, "I'm afraid I have some more bad news."

She looked up at him with wide, intense eyes that almost made him forget what he had to tell her. "Well, the bridge halfway between here and town is washed out from the storm last night. I'm afraid we can't get a tow truck up here until the water level drops."

Liz looked away, hoping he didn't see the relief in her eyes. "How long should that take?"

"No more than a day or so. I talked to the mechanic in town who's a friend of mine. As soon as the bridge is clear he'll bring the tow truck up and give me a lift back into town to get my Jeep."

Liz nodded. Another day or so. It felt like a reprieve.

Tallulah clawed delicately at Liz's hand to get her attention. Liz was grateful for the distraction, convinced Robert would see more than she wanted him to in her eyes.

"No more chocolate for you, young lady," Robert said, waggling a finger at the fat little raccoon. "You're on a diet." He laughed. "She'd eat chocolate until she exploded if I let her. She has no self control."

"I can relate to that," Liz said.

Robert grinned. "You have no self control?"

"No, I meant..." she stopped, noticing the devilish twinkle in his eye. The rising flush felt foreign on her cheeks. She hadn't blushed since she was a teenager!

Robert cleared his throat. "If you'd like I'll get some of your things from the car."

"Oh, I already got my bag while you were gone. You

said to make myself at home, so I did. I even took a bath. I hope that was all right."

"Of course," he replied. "And I do want you to feel comfortable here."

She did. Maybe too comfortable. She got up and brushed crumbs off her leggings. "That reminds me..." She reached for the travel alarm clock she'd placed on the end table. "What time is it?" she asked, starting to turn the metal key on the back.

He stood and reached for her hand, stopping her with a single word. "Don't!"

The shout sent Tallulah scrambling behind the sofa, but all Liz could think about was the way his hand felt covering hers—warm and strong and somehow possessive. She stared at his hand, the thick fingers curled around hers, remembering how tenderly they'd grazed along her skin when he'd wrapped his shirt around her. Her breath seemed to freeze in her throat as she imagined those hands touching her in other places.

"Don't?" she whispered, looking into his eyes.

He released her hand slowly. "I'm sorry. I didn't mean to frighten you. It's just...well, why do you need to know what time it is?"

She didn't have an answer. She'd never even considered it a question before. He turned away and she couldn't see his face when he spoke again.

"When the sun rises you get up and when it sets you settle in for the night. You fill each moment in between with as much as you can, enjoying it to the fullest. You don't need a clock to remind you to do that."

He turned and looked at her and she felt there was more left unsaid. She didn't question him. She was a guest in his house and it was such a small thing to ask.

She pushed the unwound clock to the back of the table, willing to suspend time—at least for now.

Robert seemed to relax, as if visibly relieved. Even Tallulah peeked out from her hiding spot, responding to the sudden lifting of tension in the air. Catching sight of the raccoon's inquisitive masked face, Liz had an idea for testing her earlier theory.

"Robert? Could you show me around your property this afternoon? Maybe we'll run into Tallulah's brothers out there." She wanted to know how far his property extended. She had to be careful, though. She already knew enough not to cross the road, and although she suspected she was safe as long as she stayed on his property, she could be wrong. Maybe the magic only extended to a small circumference around the cottage. What if they went beyond the range of the cottage's enchantment and she began aging before his eyes?

He smiled. "I'd love that. As a matter of fact, why don't we pack a picnic lunch and make a day of it?" Then he eyed her sweater and frowned. "Except you're not exactly dressed for hiking. Why don't you change back into jeans and that flannel shirt?"

There was a gleam in his eye when he mentioned the shirt and she wondered if he was remembering covering her with it this morning. *She* certainly was. Again she felt herself blushing as her body responded to his suggestion, a shiver of desire rippling through her.

"I'll be right back," she said.

* * *

When she returned dressed more appropriately for the outdoors, he was just closing the lid on a wicker picnic basket. He slung it over his arm and reached for her hand.

"Ready?"

She laced her fingers through his and replied. "Ready as I'll ever be!"

A lazy afternoon picnic in the woods sounded delightful, but she had to remember that she had an ulterior motive for this venture.

"How much land do you have," she asked, hoping the question sounded innocent enough.

"About fifteen acres," he replied. "But since the land surrounding it is wild and untouched, it sometimes feels as if the whole mountain belongs to me. Or I belong to it." He smiled. "There's a clearing out back on the far edge of the pond. I built a small gazebo there and it's a beautiful spot to picnic. It was Elise's..."

His voice trailed off and she gave his hand an encouraging squeeze as they stepped outside into the sunlight. "It's all right. You can talk about her."

He smiled and continued, his voice softer. "It was her favorite spot. Sometimes I'd come home and find her sitting out there with a book and she'd look up and blink, as if surprised that so much time had passed."

Liz nodded. "Time has a way of sneaking up on us like that. One day you turn around and wonder where it all went."

They walked on in silence, each of them lost in their own private thoughts. Liz sneaked a peek at her hands for early warning signs as they moved away from the cottage, but so far she was still safe. There was no indication of age creeping up on her.

"Don't look now," Robert whispered, "but we're being followed."

Liz heard rustling behind them. "Which one is it?"

"Rhett," he said. "He's acting nonchalant, but he's definitely curious about you."

"Should I be frightened?"

"Not if you have dog biscuits to bribe him with."

She stopped and stared at him. "I don't."

"Well," he said with a teasing grin. "You're lucky I remembered to pack a few then, aren't you?"

She smiled back, feeling more alive than she had in years. The easy camaraderie, coupled with the natural beauty of the land around them combined to surround her with a soothing peace and the belief that time really could stand still.

"Hear that?" he said.

She cocked her head and listened, aware of a rippling, rushing sound in the distance.

He pointed to an outcropping of rock on the far edge of the pond. "Over there. The pond is fed by a mountain spring that runs down the rock face of the mountain."

Liz followed his gesture, delighted. "It's like a little waterfall."

He nodded. "We're almost there."

They rounded a bend and suddenly a clearing opened up before them. A path snaked through the glade, leading to a high-domed, octagon gazebo nestled amid a grove of aspen. Wild roses climbed the white trellised sides. The sound of the water rushing into the pond was clearer here, adding to the fairy tale setting.

"It's incredible," she said, knowing that wasn't enough. "Perfect. Absolutely perfect."

He gave a courtly bow and held out his arm. She rested her hand on his bent elbow and let him guide her up the stone step through the open wall of the gazebo. The air was fragrant with a delicate floral perfume. No wonder Elise loved it here. Liz already felt an intense affinity with this spot more than any other.

She never wanted to leave.

As if reading her thoughts, Robert held her gaze. "We have all the time in the world."

All the time in the world. As impossible as it sounded, she believed him. The thought was intoxicating. What more idyllic place to spend the rest of her life?

She reached for his hand and he lowered them both to the stone floor, leaning against the balustrade and easing her into his arms. She rested against his chest and sighed, losing herself in the magical beauty around her.

It didn't take long for Tallulah to join them, familiarity making her bold. Her brothers hung back, playing at the edges of the pond and keeping a wary eye on the gazebo. Robert reached into the picnic basket and pulled out a bag of dog biscuits. He quietly coaxed the siblings closer until all three circled the gazebo. Liz laughed as Rocky stretched and caught a biscuit Robert tossed his way. They finished the biscuits, each raccoon getting its share of affection from their surrogate father before scampering back into the forest. Liz felt a wave of tenderness as she watched the way Robert cared for the animals. They obviously adored him.

"I can't believe how affectionate they are," Liz said. "I guess I never thought of raccoons as pets."

"It's illegal in most states to keep them as pets," he explained. "Rescued babies like these little guys have to be eased back into the wild once they're old enough to survive."

He gestured at Tallulah still watching them from a distance. "She's having the hardest time of it. She's not quite ready to cut the apron strings yet, and I think she might be a little jealous of you."

Liz couldn't help thinking of her own children. How empty she'd felt when they'd finally ventured out into the world. She'd spent most of her life raising them to do just that, but along with the satisfaction of watching them grow into responsible adults there'd been a wistful sense of loss. She'd been a mother for so long she'd found it hard to define her place in the world when they left home.

Her children. Again the real world intruded as she imagined trying to explain to them this sudden impulsive desire to escape into a fantasy world. She couldn't just disappear, yet she knew they wouldn't understand if she stayed here either. She'd cave in under their outrage. It wasn't her own choice to make.

"Penny for your thoughts," Robert said softly.

She sighed. He knew so little about her and she didn't want to break the spell by telling him everything. She didn't want to see the look in his eyes change as he recast her image into that of mother and school nurse rather than a fairy tale princess dropped on his doorstep. She didn't want things to change. She didn't want to lose him. Just once she wanted to do something for herself, even if it was something no one would approve of or understand.

She snuggled into his arms. "I was just thinking how lovely it is here. Almost magical." Resting against his chest, she could feel the vibrations of his voice as he spoke.

"Magical is exactly the word I'd have chosen," he said. "Do you believe in magic? Do you believe in destiny?"

Did she? Once she had. Once upon a time, a very

long time ago. "I believe there are things we're not meant to understand or question." She formed her reply carefully, exploring her answers as if for the first time. "I believe we make our own destiny. I believe that everything happens for a reason, even if it's not immediately clear what that reason might be."

His voice was soft at her ear, his breath warm as it caressed the hollow of her neck. "Do you believe in love?"

Her answer was little more than a sigh. "Yes."

He nodded, his cheek briefly grazing hers. "Then you believe in magic."

Relaxing into his arms, she knew he was right. Love was magic—elusive and mysterious and powerful. Who was she to question magic? If she turned her back on it now, would it ever find her again?

CHAPTER SEVEN

They lunched on leftovers he'd packed—cold chicken and crusty sourdough rolls, along with slightly crushed and broken chocolate chip cookies. Her appetite surprised her and she ate with uninhibited pleasure. Then he fed her cool chunks of ripe watermelon from his fingertips, catching the sweet juice from the corners of her mouth and brushing it across her lips. She'd never tasted anything as sweet.

After lunch, they splashed barefoot along the edges of the pond. When she slipped on a wet rock and nearly tumbled, he caught her in a strong grip, lifting her off her feet and holding her against his chest, then slowly sliding her down along his body until her feet touched the ground. She pressed against him, her knees weak, her heart pounding.

She held her breath, knowing he would kiss her. Wanting him to kiss her. The moment stretched and expanded, the air around them ripening with magic. Slowly he tipped her chin upward, moving closer. He brushed his lips across hers, the merest whisper of a caress. Her lips parted with a silent gasp of pleasure which drew his breath into her soul. She captured his magic and held it deep within her, taking a little piece of him as her own and giving her own breath back in return.

They broke apart slowly and he cradled her head to

his chest. Her lips were warm with the imprint of his kiss as she rested her cheek against his pounding heartbeat. He held her close and she felt something essential slip into place, as if she'd finally found what she'd given up searching for.

Robert's calm exterior was in stark contrast to the inner turmoil he felt as conflicting emotions assaulted him. Emotions he both fought and welcomed at one and the same time. He felt walls crumbling, passions stirring, fresh yearnings warring with ancient vows.

Above all he was frightened to love, only to lose again. It was safer to hang onto a ghost than to risk being alive and vulnerable. But the harder he struggled, the more he fell under the captivating charm of this woman who'd stepped into his world. It was as if a window had opened, casting blinding light on eyes that had grown accustomed to the dark.

Releasing her, he bent and picked up a rock, looking for a distraction. With a smooth snap of his wrist, he sent the flat rock skimming and skipping over the surface of the pond. It bounced and hopped, leaving a string of rippled pearls along the water's surface.

Beside him, Liz reached for a rock and flung it across the pond. It flew through the air and hit with a splashing plunk, sinking immediately.

He chuckled at her frown of disappointment, then searched for a more appropriate rock and showed her how to hold the flat disc, curling her thumb and index finger around the smooth edge. "Like this," he said, bringing his arm out perpendicular to his side and flicking it expertly across the pond.

She tried again and again, refusing to give up until

she finally managed a victorious triple hop. Her laughter was as pure and sweet as the bubbling spring water, a sound he knew he'd never grow tired of.

They collapsed at the edge of the pond, talking quietly as he told her how he'd built the cottage. Liz urged him to share memories which hadn't seen the light of day in so long they almost seemed to belong to someone else.

He was surprised to find himself smiling as the memories resurfaced, unlocking hidden places in his heart which had previously been too painful to revisit. Elise collecting river rocks while he and Herb poured concrete for the foundation, the elk and deer which ambled by each morning as if to check their progress. He remembered everything, from the way the sun slanted through the Blue Spruce and Douglas Firs in the evening, to how the air smelled, crisp and new in the morning.

"It must have been an incredible project," Liz said. In her gentle way, she encouraged him with a nod, a squeeze of his hand, and filled the empty spaces between sentences with understanding.

"It was a labor of love. We planned to spend the rest of our lives here." The words weren't as painful as he'd imagined they would be. For the first time he could look back on the time they had together without railing at the injustice of losing her too soon.

"Elise was...magical. She filled every corner of the cottage with her own unique beauty." He closed his eyes for a moment, taking a slow, deep breath. "I see her in every room, every nook and cranny. I promised her I would never change a thing and I've kept that promise to this day."

Liz touched his hand, assuring him without words.

He knew she'd understand. Most people didn't. Even Herb and Janie thought it might be easier if he were to make a fresh start. But he couldn't leave the cottage. He couldn't abandon Elise that way.

Without even realizing he was doing it, Robert reached out and tugged Liz closer until her head rested against his shoulder, drawing solace he'd denied himself for so long.

They sat in comfortable silence for a long time, neither one ready or willing to break the spell. Only when he felt shiver did he realize it was getting cool. Night would be falling soon.

"We'd better get back," he said, helping her to her feet.

"Where does that trail go," she asked, pointing to a path that led through the woods away from the cottage.

"There's a natural cave formation along an old Indian trail out that way," he explained. "Would you like to explore it?" he asked.

Her eyes lit up and she squeezed his hand. "Can we?"

"Not tonight. It'll be getting dark soon and I don't want to take a chance on losing you." The words brought a catch to his throat, but she didn't seem to notice.

Twilight deepened the shadows of the woods as they started home. *Home.* Suddenly the word was laden with meaning. It hadn't really felt like home in a long time. He didn't want to hope that she might one day think of the cottage as home too.

"Liz?"

She looked up at him. "Yes?"

What did he want to say? *Don't leave? Stay here with me.* He couldn't. It was impulsive, rash, and there were still so many things left unsaid.

He took her hand and raised it to his lips. "Thank you," he said. "Thank you for the pleasure of your company."

She gave a slight curtsy and smiled. "You're very welcome."

* * *

The cottage was layered in darkness when they returned. Robert lit a candle, but the soft glow enhanced rather than dispelled the shadows. Suddenly Liz felt vulnerable. Vulnerable to her own desires. The room was too intimate, the cottage too isolated, the situation too intense with possibilities. She felt on the brink of making a decision that could alter her life and knew she wasn't qualified to make a choice at this moment when passion overruled logic.

She crossed her arms in front of herself while Robert lit more candles. She had to think. She had to think clearly. She had to...

"Are you cold?" he asked, concern softening his voice.

"No." She laughed, a high, quivering sound that laid bare her nervousness.

A frown creased his forehead. She thought for a moment he was going to reach out and felt herself withdraw from him.

As if sensing her discomfort, he checked his movement and stepped away. "Why don't I make us some coffee?" he suggested.

"Yes." She nodded, reduced to monosyllables as the tension ebbed and swelled around them. What was she doing? Whatever was happening between them couldn't be denied. It was real. It was unmistakable. And it was intense. She knew if she gave in to her feelings there'd be no going back. What could she give him afterward? There was no future for them, nowhere to go from here.

She looked around. This room, this whole cottage, was a shrine to his wife's memory. Every nook and cranny vibrated with remembrance. He'd said so himself. There was no place for another woman's touch here. No place for her.

Yet she knew if he touched her in the darkness, if he called her name she'd rush to him and never look back. That's what frightened her most. She had to keep her sanity. She had to keep her distance. It was up to her to be the mature, responsible one.

Just then the lights flickered twice, then stayed on, filling the room with a cheerful brightness. She took a deep breath, feeling some of the tension lift.

Robert peeked into the room. "Well, at least the power's back. Want to check the phones while I get our coffee?"

She nodded and reached for the phone on the end table. The line was noisy with static, but there was no dial tone. "Still no luck," she called out.

He came in carrying two steaming mugs of coffee. The familiar, everyday aroma in the brightly-lit room made her fears seem silly and groundless. She'd simply gotten caught up in the moment, that was all. She'd forgotten the real world, a real world of coffee and bright lights and hospitality.

He handed her the mug and stayed within touching distance. She blew on the steamy liquid, avoiding his eyes. She felt rather than saw him move away. He sat in a wing back chair beside the stone fireplace and she moved to the furthest end of the couch, tucking her legs beneath her and holding tight to the mug to keep her hands from shaking.

The silence stretched between them, jarring in its uncomfortable stillness.

He cleared his throat. "Liz. For a minute there before the lights came on. You seemed...frightened." He rushed on, as if needing to get the words out before she could stop him. "I would never—"

She shushed him. "Oh Robert. I know. I know." She took a deep breath and released it slowly, feeling the tension ease from her shoulders. "It's not you. I was just feeling confused. Things are moving too fast."

"Too fast? I told you we have all the time in the world."

"Do we?" she asked.

He waited, but she didn't know what else to say. She didn't have all the time in the world. She'd have to leave eventually.

Neither spoke. The silence stretched between them, becoming almost suffocating. She missed his smile, his easy laughter, but didn't know how to coax it back.

He reached for the guitar leaning against the fireplace and began strumming softly, easing the stillness back into the shadowy corners. Setting her coffee on the table, she leaned her head against the cushion and closed her eyes, letting the strains of the guitar soothe the tension from her mind and body. Her hands relaxed in her lap and her breathing deepened.

Occasionally she'd seem to catch a wisp of a familiar tune, but for the most part the melody was elusive. Elusive yet compelling, bewitching her into a trance-like calm as his fingers coaxed sweet magic from the strings.

She drifted, losing herself in the mood he created, drifting deeper and deeper as the haunting melody settled like a soft blanket around her, weaving its way into her dreams.

She was floating, rising soft and warm and peaceful to the heavens. As she drifted slowly upward, a gentle resistance held her back, tugging her back to earth. She felt helpless, trapped between here and there.

Part of her consciousness watched the dream unfold, lucid and aware that she was dreaming, yet unable to wake up. She recognized a familiar sense of melding, aware of another presence. She felt thoughts brush against her own, expanding and drifting outward like ripples on the pond. Still she went deeper, searching for answers she knew lurked beneath the surface.

* * *

Robert watched Liz sleep. He knew he should wake her, but couldn't take his eyes off her face, so peaceful in slumber. It was only when her forehead creased into a frown and she began mumbling in her sleep that he shook her shoulder gently.

"Let go," she mumbled. "Please, you have to let me go."

He drew back, surprised. "Liz? Wake up. You're dreaming."

She opened her eyes halfway, still caught in the grip of a dream. "Robert. I have to tell you something."

"What is it?"

"I don't know." Her voice trailed off in a sleepy yawn ending in a half sigh. "But I think...it's important."

He brushed a wisp of hair from her forehead and

smiled. "If it's important you'll remember in the morning."

"Morning," she repeated, but instead of getting up she only sank deeper into the cushions, nuzzling her face against the arm of the sofa.

"You'll hate me if I let you sleep like that all night," he warned her.

"Okay," she mumbled, not moving.

Without thinking, he gathered her up in his arms, holding her against his chest. Her arms came around his neck as he cradled her, warm and sleepy and so soft, in his embrace. She tucked her face under his chin and he felt her lips move soundlessly against his neck, her eyelashes fluttered once along his skin. He thought his heart would explode with tenderness as he carried her to her room and laid her on the bed. He tucked her in, tucking the covers around her.

"Sleep now, precious," he whispered, stroking her cheek.

She nestled into the pillows and sighed. Her hand slipped out from beneath the blanket, thumb tucked between the first two fingers of her curled fist. His breath caught in his throat. It was exactly the way Elise had always slept.

"Robert," she mumbled. "Promise me..."

He took a step backward, his mind reeling. With those few words she'd torn through the fragile web he'd spun around bruised and tender memories. As he stared, her image began to blend and meld, overlaid with night shadows and phantom memories. For a moment it was Elise there, then he blinked and she was gone. Only her voice remained, drifting out of the darkness.

"Promise me, please?"

He said the only thing he could. "I promise."

Then he turned and strode out of the room, leaving the ghostly echoes of the past behind him.

CHAPTER EIGHT

Liz struggled upward from a deep sleep. Her limbs were heavy, her head dull. The sheets and blankets were a tangled testament to a restless night, which had left her groggy and lethargic.

There was a dull, rhythmic pounding coming from somewhere. At first she thought it was the first, tentative footsteps of an approaching migraine, then realized the sound came from outside. She padded to the open window and saw Robert chopping wood in the distance. He'd taken his shirt off and his skin glistened as he raised the ax high then swung it with a singing swoosh, splitting cleanly into the wood. Chips flew in all directions and the ax gave a soft squeal as he twisted it from the creamy wedge.

His muscles rippled in the sunlight and a small grunt escaped his lips as he drove the ax deeper. There seemed to be more to his efforts than simply stacking firewood. Liz wondered if he used physical labor to fight off other demons.

She couldn't take her gaze from him. There was something so sensual about the way his body moved, his legs planted apart, hips lifting to accommodate the shifting weight of the swinging ax. His body tensed and released with each downward thrust, over and over again like a perfectly choreographed dance.

Another sound assaulted her. She looked around,

blinking. It took a moment to realize the phone was ringing. The sound seemed so alien here in the cottage. She glanced at the doorway, then back to Robert outside chopping wood, apparently unaware of the jangling phone. She ran to the living room and snatched up the receiver.

"Hello?"

There was a pause on the other end, then surprisingly she heard her own name. "Elizabeth?"

"Yes?" *Who knew she was here?* She cupped her hand around the receiver. "Who is this?"

"Oh," the man said. "This is Robert's friend Herb at the garage. He told me about your car breaking down."

That explained it. She let out a breath. "He's outside," she said, secretly pleased that Robert had mentioned her by name. "Cutting wood. Shall I get him?"

"Nope. I was calling to say the road is clear and I can get that tow truck out to you this afternoon."

Her shoulders slumped. So soon? If her car was fixed, she had no reason to stay. Now that the phones were working again she should check in with her family so they wouldn't worry. There was a tug at her soul as the real world pulled her back.

"Ma'am?"

She realized he was waiting for an answer. What should she tell him? If he brought the tow truck to fix her car, she'd have to cross that road—literally, as well as figuratively. How could she get around that? She didn't want Robert to see her stripped of her youth. Not without warning him first. She needed a little more time to get up the courage, to prepare herself for the end.

"Herman?"

"It's Herb, ma'am," he corrected her.

"I'm sorry." The term "ma'am" made her feel ancient, but she refused to let it rattle her as she searched for a way out. She remembered Robert's promise to show her the old Indian trail and explore the caves. "Herb, I'm not sure we're going to be here this afternoon."

"That's not a problem," he said. "Just leave the keys in the glove compartment. I'll pull you out of that ditch and charge the battery up for you. We'll have you on your way in no time."

Liz started to argue, then realized they did things differently here. People trusted each other. They left their door unlocked so the raccoons could help themselves to the pantry, their keys were safe in the glove compartment of their car, and neighbors helped each other.

As if to confirm her assessment, he continued. "If I see anything that could be a problem I'll just tow it back to the garage. Otherwise you can swing by on your way back to town and settle with me."

"How will I find you?" she asked.

He chuckled. "Coldwater Springs isn't all that big. I'm the only garage in town."

It wasn't a perfect solution, but it would buy her some time. She thanked him and hung up. Outside Robert was still splitting wood and she had one more phone call to make.

She opened her purse and pulled out her cell phone, disappointed that there was still no signal. Well, at least Robert's land line was working. She dialed her daughter's number, keeping an eye on the door in case Robert came back inside. She'd have to make this quick.

Marcie picked up on the second ring. "Mom, where have you been? I've been trying to call your cell phone."

"I'm in the mountains. There's no reception up here.."

"What mountains? I thought I'd hear from you by now."

"The Rocky Mountains. Colorado. I'll explain later, but I'm fine. Now, why have you been trying to reach me?"

"I just wanted to make sure you were all right. And to talk. The baby..."

A spike of fear hit her. "What's wrong with the baby?"

"Nothing, really. I mean, he's not sleeping much and I'm not sure if he's getting enough formula and sometimes he just cries and cries and I don't know what to do. I just needed to hear your voice and to have you tell me that's normal."

Liz smiled. "Oh honey. That's about as normal as can be. New babies adapt better than new mothers. Pretty soon the two of you will settle into a routine and you'll start to recognize his different cries and know when he's hungry or tired or just wants to be snuggled and rocked."

Marcie sighed at the other end. Liz wanted to reach out and hug her. She wanted to tell Marcie that as a parent she'd make mistakes along the way, and worry more nights than she could count, and wonder if she could have done things better. Those fears would never end because parenting was a life-long job whose qualifications changed as children grew and moved away. One thing never changed, however. The love and support that nurtured them would always be there, a touchstone to guide them for the rest of their lives.

"Honey," she said. "You're a wonderful mother and a loving, caring person. You're doing fine."

"I get scared, Mom. What if I mess up? He's so tiny and he depends on me for everything."

"Would it surprise you to know I still get scared and worry about you kids? That's what mothers do. We worry. After awhile you learn not to worry so much about the little things and save it for the really big things. Wait till he gets his license!"

Marcie laughed. Although Liz could hear the exhaustion in her voice, she knew her daughter would be fine.

"Where are you heading from there?" Marcy asked.

"I'm, uh...well, I'm going to stay here in Colorado for a few more days." She tried not to feel guilty about her decision. It was her vacation and there was no rush to get back.

"Where can I reach you?" Marcie asked.

Liz wasn't sure what to say. She couldn't give Marcie Robert's number. And she realized that once her car was fixed she'd have no rational excuse to stay here anyway.

"Hold on," she said. She dug into her purse and found the receipt for the Bed and Breakfast she'd stayed at back in Coldwater Springs. Was it only two nights ago? It seemed almost like another life, another person.

She read the number off to Marcie and told her she could be reached there in an emergency, at least for a few more days. She wasn't sure beyond that. She wasn't sure of anything except the fact that she wasn't ready to go home yet.

She felt a tug of guilt when she hung up, but another part of her mind argued that she had a right to just this once do something that made *her* happy. She wasn't hurting anyone, was she?

Suddenly she realized the sounds of chopping wood outside had stopped. She ran her fingers through her hair and remembered she was still wearing the rumpled clothes she'd slept in last night. It was too late to change, though. She barely had time to run a comb through her hair, wash her face and brush her teeth before she heard him coming in.

He carried an armload of firewood and filled the wood bin beside the fireplace. "Morning, sleepyhead," he called out as she emerged from the bathroom.

"I don't usually sleep this late," she apologized. "It must be this fresh mountain air."

His shirt was still off and she wanted to touch him, run her hands along the back of his neck and shoulders and ease the knots from his muscles. She wanted to feel the sunlight warm on his skin.

He stacked the wood, his back to her, then straightened and turned. "You had a rough night."

Had she? She didn't remember.

He glanced at her open purse. "Are you leaving?" There was a bantering tone to his voice, but the smile on his face didn't reach his eyes.

"Leaving? No. I was just looking for something." Flustered, she searched for an excuse, finally pulling a pen from her purse. "I was going to leave you a note telling you I was going for a morning walk."

His eyes narrowed suspiciously. "A note? I was right outside."

"Yes, but you were busy chopping wood." She could see he wasn't buying her hasty excuse.

He moved lazily toward her, closing the distance between them. Their gazes locked and time seemed to stand still. Her heartbeat quickened with each step that brought him closer, until he stood before her and she could feel the heat from his body, the undeniable magnetism of him.

He reached out and took the pen from her hand. "There's no need to leave me a note. I'm right here now."

He was so close there barely seemed room for a whisper between them, so she merely nodded. She fumbled for words, trying not to stare at his bare skin, but her hand moved with a will of its own, gently wiping a bead of sweat trickling down the center of his chest with the pad of her thumb. Her open palm rested against his heart and he reached up and held her hand tight to his chest until she could feel his heartbeat calling to hers, twin pulses merging into one perfect, beating rhythm.

When he spoke again, his voice was so soft she had to lean closer to hear him. "If you don't mind waiting for me to shower, I could join you on that walk."

That reminded her of the phone call. The man from the garage would be coming by this afternoon and she wanted them to be far away when he showed up. Should she tell Robert the phones were working now? No, he might offer to call the garage for her. She'd tell him while they were away.

"Could we explore that trail today?"

"If you'd like," he said. "Let me get cleaned up and we'll plan our afternoon."

When he stepped away, she wanted to call him back. She missed his nearness. "Robert?"

He turned back and raised an eyebrow, waiting.

"Have you eaten yet?" she asked.

A slow smile curled his lips and he shook his head. "I'm not used to anyone caring whether I've eaten."

She looked away. "I just thought maybe you'd worked up an appetite."

"Oh, I have, little darlin'," and with a roguish grin he

turned and walked away, leaving her to wonder if he really meant what she thought he did.

She smiled and watched him walk away, admiring the smooth movements of his body, then rushed off to the kitchen before he could turn around again and catch the quick flush of desire on her face.

In the kitchen she scoured the pantry, lining up cooking ingredients while she listened to the sound of water running. The harder she tried not to think of him standing naked under the running water, the stronger the vision became, until her hands were trembling as she cracked eggs into a bowl of corn meal and flour.

"Get a grip on yourself," she murmured, taking a slow, deep breath. She preheated the oven and turned the batter into muffin tins. She was a messy cook, leaving bowls and measuring cups scattered along the counter. Lids leaned crookedly on canisters hastily pushed aside to make room for a mixing bowl twice as large as she needed. Batter dripped down the side of the bowl and onto the counter.

But all the bustling around the kitchen didn't help take her mind off the effect he had on her—an effect heightened when the water stopped running and she imagined him stepping naked from the shower and towel drying his long, lean body.

She had his coffee waiting for him when he entered the kitchen wearing a fresh pair of Levi's and a white, sleeveless T-shirt that clung provocatively to his damp chest.

"Your turn," he said, taking the cup from her hands. "I'll finish up here."

She turned kitchen duty over to him and headed for the bathroom where he'd laid out fresh towels for her.

She stepped into the tub before filling it and closed her eyes feeling him in the molecules of the air. The moist steam caressed her naked skin. She wondered if her feet were in the same spot his had just been. Her knees weak, she slid down, sitting in the tub for a moment, before turning on the faucet and letting the warm water cover her hot skin.

Was it as hard for him to imagine her in here bathing as it had been for her? She rubbed the washcloth briskly along her skin trying to scrub the erotic thoughts from her mind and body, but they wouldn't leave. Dipping her head beneath the surface, she washed her hair, then wrung the water from it. When she stepped out of the tub, she twisted the clean towel around her hair and reached for the still-damp towel he'd left hanging on the towel rack, using it to dry the rest of her body. The sensation was intensely erotic and brought a tingling flush to her skin.

Her hair was still damp when she dressed and returned to the kitchen just as he was pulling the corn muffins from the oven. The air was thick with the aromas of breakfast, but her appetite had been stimulated for more than food.

"Just in time," he said, handing her a cup of coffee.

She took the cup from his hand and looked around the kitchen. He'd cleaned up and put everything back where it belonged. Other than the smell of warm muffins rising from the oven, there was no sign that she'd been there.

No sign at all.

CHAPTER NINE

Robert knew something had changed. He'd catch her frowning, as if struggling over a nagging puzzle. They ate in the casual silence of sentences which faded away without follow-up, the way strangers talked at bus stops. He couldn't help feeling he'd done something wrong, but for the life of him couldn't figure out what it was. As they cleaned up, she seemed to be challenging him, deliberately putting things back in the wrong place. He could feel her moving further and further away.

He thought exploring the caves would lighten her mood, but they never even got that far. Halfway along the trail she stopped.

"I can't," she said, her voice quivering.

Even shaded in the canopy of trees he could see fear in her eyes. "What's wrong?" He reached for her hand, which trembled in his. "Liz?"

"I just can't," she sobbed and he was horrified to see tears in her eyes before she turned and ran back along the path.

He followed more slowly, giving her some privacy without leaving her completely alone. He felt helpless, powerless to bring the smile back to her face. It didn't surprise him to find her at the gazebo. It did surprise him to see how forlorn she looked huddled on the floor of the gazebo. He watched, hidden in the forest's shadows of the forest, grateful when Tallulah waddled over and curled on Liz's lap, giving her the comfort he couldn't.

Liz stroked the animal's pelt, her face a study in misery. From where he stood he could see the shimmer of tears on her cheeks and it nearly broke his heart. He tried to read her lips as she poured her heart out to the raccoon, but couldn't tell what she was saying. Tallulah seemed to understand, though. She stretched up, clasping a tiny forepaw on either side of Liz's face, and gave her a tiny, nibbling kiss.

Liz knew she was being irrational but couldn't stop herself. First there was that unexpected surge of jealousy this morning when Robert had erased every trace of her presence in the cottage, putting things back exactly the way Elise would want it. She knew she could never replace Elise's memory. She wouldn't want to. No one would ever replace her husband's memory either, but she could find a place in her heart for another love without feeling as if she'd betrayed his memory. By the same token, she didn't want to replace Elise, but she suspected there was no place in the cottage or the rest of Robert's world for another woman.

That was the irrational part. No matter how hard she tried to shuffle the pieces of their lives around, there was no way to fit them together. They came from two different worlds and neither could exist in the other's time or space. So why did it hurt to know he couldn't make room for her in his life?

Because she was falling in love with him.

It didn't make sense. It shouldn't have happened. Yet there was no denying it. She was falling madly, passionately, desperately in love with him. Looking back she could see that it had started the moment she'd seen the compassion with which he'd wrapped her watch and put it in a safe place. It had blossomed slowly as each layer peeled away, revealing more of the man behind the walls he'd erected to protect his heart. If anything, his loyalty to his wife's memory made him even more dear to her.

But she didn't want to share him with a perfect ghost.

As if all that confusion wasn't enough, she'd felt the transformation coming over her on the trail. She should have asked whether the caves were on his property, but she hadn't thought to. Not until it was too late.

She'd started to feel a little weak at first, her breath more shallow. Then she'd noticed an ache in her calves, but had chalked it up to the hike up the mountain trail. If she hadn't been struggling with her emotions, she might have noticed the warning signs sooner. By the time she did, it was almost too late. She'd managed to turn Robert around before he'd glimpsed her turning older before his eyes, thanks in part to the sheltered darkness of the forest.

But how long could she hide it from him? What if she decided to give everything up for love—her children, her friends, her job. What if she gave everything up to live here with Robert? How long before the cottage began to feel like a prison? How long could she hide her real face from him?

Tallulah was a great listener, but didn't have any answers. When the raccoon cradled a tiny paw on either side of her face and rubbed noses in a little raccoon kiss, Liz felt as if her heart would break. "Us girls have to stick together," she whispered.

A long, lean shadow fell over the gazebo steps. "I

know I'm not as cute," he said, "but could I have one of those kisses? Please?"

Liz didn't look up, knowing one look in his eyes and all her resistance would crumble. "You'll have to ask Tallulah," she said.

"I'd rather have a kiss from you." His voice was so soft, so tender Liz nearly lost her resolve.

Tallulah stood like a bodyguard between them, facing Robert with an angry, scolding chirp. Liz bowed her head, hiding the beginnings of a smile. *You tell him, girl.*

Robert sighed. "I don't seem to be very popular with the ladies today." He reached into his pocket, knelt and unwrapped a square of chocolate. With an almost apologetic glance at Liz, Tallulah swiped the treat and retreated to a corner to eat it in guilty silence.

Traitor! Liz realized she couldn't depend on a hungry raccoon with a weakness for chocolate to fight her battles for her. She felt Robert move closer, but still wouldn't meet his gaze.

He held out a square of chocolate, offering it to her. "I guess it would be too much to expect this to work twice, huh?"

This time she couldn't stop the smile that played around the corners of her lips. *Why did he have to be so damn adorable?*

"It has nuts," he coaxed.

She had to bite her bottom lip to keep back the retort bubbling to the surface. Slowly she reached for the chocolate and raised her eyes to his. A world of emotions seemed to pass between their locked gaze.

He reached out his hand and held it there, waiting patiently until she placed hers in his strong grasp. He knelt beside her and gently pulled her into his arms. "I'm sorry," he whispered.

"For what?"

"I don't know. Can't I just be sorry and leave it at that?"

While Liz thought about it, Tallulah crept over and stole the square of chocolate from her hand. She felt Robert's lips brush across her forehead and settled into his arms. He held her quietly, which was exactly what she needed.

"Robert?"

He'd grown so used to the silence that when she called his name it startled him. He'd been content to just hold her, afraid if he spoke he'd say the wrong thing. "Yes?"

"I have to tell you something. I should have told you before, but I wanted us to have this time together before the real world intruded." She stopped, as if getting the string of words out had exhausted her.

He brushed his fingers through her hair, waiting for her to work up the nerve for whatever it was she wanted to say.

She turned in his arms and faced him. "The phones are working now. Hugh called."

"Hugh?"

"Your friend from the garage..."

"Ahhh. Herb."

"Yes, Herb. He said the road was clear enough to bring the tow truck up this afternoon. I didn't want to spoil our outing."

He simply nodded, holding her a little tighter, a little closer.

"Anyway," she continued. "He said he'd probably have the car running before we got back. I know I should have told you, but I wanted us to have some time alone before I left."

"You're leaving?" He studied her face. "Why?"

She lowered her gaze, then looked up, pleading with him to understand. "How would it look? There's no reason for me to stay here anymore. It would be, um...inappropriate."

"To whom?" he asked.

She shrugged. "I don't know. I just don't feel right. I've reserved a room at Stone Haven for tonight."

"And then what?" He was afraid to ask, but he needed to know.

"I don't know," she replied. "Where do we go from here?"

"I don't know either." He cradled her head to his chest and whispered. "Just don't leave, please. If you leave we'll never have the chance to find out."

CHAPTER TEN

They held each other and talked as the afternoon sunlight slanted into the gazebo, eventually coming to a compromise. She agreed to stay another day, but insisted on moving her things back to the bed and breakfast in town. He was disappointed and she was adamant. What she didn't tell him was that she didn't trust herself spending the night alone with him.

When they arrived back at the cottage her car was pulled into the driveway. Even though she'd made the decision to leave, she wasn't prepared for the feelings that assaulted her now that she actually could.

"Looks like your car's fixed," he said, no hint of emotion in his voice or on his face.

She nodded, not sure exactly what to say. He seemed to retreat back into the safety of solitude, but she could feel him watching her as she packed her things, moving silently around the cottage until there was no evidence that she'd been there at all.

He only interrupted her once to ask if she would like to stay for dinner. She knew that dinner would lead to coffee in front of the fire, and then to soft music and darkness enveloping them in an intimacy which she might not be strong enough to fight. She had to escape in the light of day while she still had some resolve left.

"They're holding a room for me at Stone Haven," she

said, as if that made any difference. "And I want to get into town before it gets too dark and I get lost again."

He took the suitcase from her hand and carried it to the car. Liz was grateful the mechanic had moved the car into the driveway so she didn't have to worry about stepping outside the magical periphery of the cottage. Otherwise she might have had to sneak out in the middle of the night while Robert was sleeping.

He leaned against the driver's door, barring her from getting in the car. "Will I see you again?" he asked.

"You have the number for Stone Haven, right?"

"Yes, but that doesn't answer my question."

She didn't meet his eyes. She couldn't lie. She had a feeling that she'd return to her senses the further she moved away from the cottage. If that happened she didn't want to be bound by promises that would only pull them both deeper into an impossible situation.

He stepped aside. For a moment neither of them moved, as she hovered on the brink of decision. The sun glinted off the side mirror, sharp and silvery brittle. Their reflections hovered motionless in the car window, like shadowy statues. Liz reached for a business card tucked under the windshield wiper, the movement giving her the momentum she needed to break out of her daze. She stared at the card, the words "Herb's Garage and Automotive" in block letters beneath a smeared grease print.

"Could you do me a favor?" Robert asked, running his finger over the card in her hand. "Would you stop by and let Herb take a closer look at the car before you leave Coldwater Springs?"

That sounded enough like a dismissal to make her reach out and open the car door. "I will," she said, forcing a smile to her face.

* * *

Robert watched her car until it wound out of sight, afraid it might be the last he'd ever see of her. What if she just kept driving, never looking back? How could he have let her go so easily? He turned back to the cottage and saw Tallulah sitting on the porch rail, staring at him with what looked like accusation on her masked face.

He shrugged. "I asked her not to leave. What else could I do?" The raccoon only stared back, then turned and waddled away. Robert stormed inside, slamming the door behind him and muttering. "I don't know why I should have to explain myself to a raccoon anyway."

Once inside, he would have welcomed even the raccoon's scolding. It was too quiet, too empty. He turned on the radio, but it mocked him, playing *Stardust*. He remembered his first sight of Liz standing in the doorway humming the tune and her bashful smile when she opened her eyes and caught him watching her. With an angry twist of the knob he turned off the radio.

Still the melody taunted him, haunting lyrics weaving through his thoughts of Liz. He walked through the cottage, straightening doilies, plumping cushions, taking the sugar bowl which Liz had moved to the table this morning and putting it back on the counter where Elise had always kept it. Only when everything was perfectly aligned and in place did he allow himself to relax in the smothering silence.

He reached for the phone and dialed Herb's number. Liz might run from him, but he knew she wouldn't go without taking care of her obligations first. She'd stop by the garage and pay Herb for towing her car. Plus she'd promised him she'd let Herb look at it before leaving town. He knew she'd keep that promise.

Now he'd extract his second promise today—this time from a friend he knew he could count on to watch over Liz for as long as she decided to stay in town.

* * *

Liz didn't like the sound the car was making. At first she'd blamed the rattling on bone-crunching bounces over the dirt ruts, but the metallic clanking grew louder as she got closer to town. The accident must have shaken something loose. She only hoped it wasn't anything serious.

Liz decided to make Herb's Garage and Automotive her first stop. It was easy enough to find, at the second traffic light along Main Street, only half a block from Stone Haven.

A bell over the door announced her entrance, and Herb came out of the back wiping his hands on a red bandanna, which he then shoved into his back pocket. She knew it was Herb because his name was embroidered over the pocket of his work shirt. Since hers wasn't, she was surprised when he called her by name.

It must have shown on her face because he smiled and explained. "Robert told me you'd be stopping by. He described you, although he hardly did you justice."

He didn't give her a chance to respond to the compliment, pointing out the full-length windows of the garage office. "Besides," he said. "I recognized your car. I promised Robert I'd give it a check-up before letting you take it any farther."

She was speechless from both the compliment and the pleasure she felt knowing Robert had called ahead to ask his friend to check out her car. Herb took charge, filling the silence. "I've called Amanda over at Stone Haven and she's holding your room, so there's no rush to get there. I'd be pleased if you'd join me and the Missus for dinner since you're alone here in town."

"Oh, I couldn't," Liz began.

Herb waved off her refusal. "Of course you can. Besides, you'd be doing me a favor. Janie keeps forgetting the kids have all left home. She cooks enough food to feed an army and I end up eating leftovers all week."

His good-humored insistence put her completely at ease. "I know the feeling," she admitted. "I still haven't gotten the knack of cooking for one."

"Then it's settled," he said, turning the sign on the door from "open" to "closed" and reaching for his keys. "And you can keep Janie company while I check out your car after dinner."

* * *

Janie was delightfully bubbly and charming. Liz knew small towns were notorious for both their hospitality and gossip, but when Herb introduced her as "Robert's friend," Janie didn't bat an eye. Liz relaxed over a dinner of barbecued ribs and cole slaw. Although Herb coaxed her to eat up, when they were finished they hadn't even made a dent in the platters of food on the table.

Herb groaned mockingly. "Damn. Leftovers again! We'll have to start inviting half the town to dinner unless you get the hang of cooking for two, hon." He'd changed out of his greasy overalls for dinner and their light-hearted banter made Liz feel completely at ease. Watching their comfortable closeness, Liz realized how much she missed being half of a couple, finishing the other person's sentences, groaning over old jokes grown stale with time, and knowing there would be someone waiting at the door to greet you. Margaret Meade once said that one of the oldest human needs is having someone wonder where you are when you don't come home at night.

When Herb gave his wife a kiss on the forehead and went back to the garage, Liz and Janie found how much they had in common over butter cookies and herbal tea. Mostly they talked about their children. It felt good not to have to worry about what she said or fear giving her real age away. If anything it convinced her how impossible it would be to maintain the illusion of youth over any length of time.

Sharing motherhood stories with Janie made Liz realize something else. Robert was still young enough to want a family. It wasn't unheard of for women her age to have a baby, but she had already raised her family. It wasn't something she wanted to start over, and she would be denying him the future possibility of being a father.

As if sensing her thoughts of Robert, Janie interrupted. "How long have you known Robert?" she asked.

Liz shook her head. "Not...only a few days. He insisted I stay there when my car broke down in the storm the other night." Before she had to explain further, she turned the question around to Janie. "How long have you known him?"

"It's a small town," Janie said. "Everyone has known everyone forever."

"So, you knew Elise?"

A slow smile spread across Janie's face. "Yes. She was so beautiful. Inside and out." Janie sighed. "They were so perfect together. Like the prince and princess of some fairy tale."

"Robert said Elise loved fairy tales."

Janie nodded. "I think she really believed life held all the magic and wonder of fairy tales. And somehow when you were with her, she made you believe too."

Liz heard again the wistful tone in Robert's voice when he'd asked if she believed in magic. She had no magic to offer him. She couldn't replace the beauty and wonder he'd lost. She couldn't rewrite his fairy tale no matter how hard she tried.

They both looked up when Herb returned. He shook his head at Liz's questioning gaze and asked her whether she wanted the good news or bad news first.

"What's the bad news?" she asked, holding her breath.

"Well," he drawled. "Looks like you're gonna be needin' a new muffler."

"Oh, that's not too bad." Liz allowed herself to breathe again. She'd been afraid it was much worse. A muffler could be replaced easily.

"That wasn't the bad news," Herb said. "The bad news is I don't have one in stock that'll fit your car.

"Oh. How long...?"

"A day, maybe two," he said with a shrug.

Do you believe in destiny? She shook Robert's voice from her head. This wasn't destiny. It wasn't fate. It was an accident, that's all. It simply meant extending her trip a little longer while she explored the charming town of Coldwater Springs and tried not to do anything stupid.

* * *

Robert couldn't sleep. It took him a while to realize that the noise he was hearing was the sound of his own blood rushing through his ears. It was too damn quiet. He had to get out.

He slipped on a T-shirt and jeans and went outside for a walk. The night was clear and cool, the sky a canopy of black velvet sprinkled with stardust. The woods, which used to give him solace, now only magnified his isolation. He walked with his head down, watching the path in front of him while his mind wandered beyond the woods, into town. He wondered what Liz was doing tonight. Was she thinking of him, or was she already making plans to get away? Why had she entered his life only to leave him more discontent when she left? It wasn't fair. He'd grown accustomed to being alone. Now it wasn't enough anymore.

When he reached the glade, he looked up. Moonlight shimmered over the gazebo, giving it a celestial glow. The image blurred and wavered. He thought he saw movement, as if the moonlight were swaying to night music in the twilight shadows of the gazebo. He stepped closer.

The contours of light shifted and defined themselves into a luminous image. The drape of a gown. The gentle cascade of hair. A spectral hand hovering over the pages of a book. A breeze rustling the leaves mimicked the sound of pages turning.

Liz? Had she come back?

He moved closer, stealthy and silent in the muted hush of the forest. Only his heart cried out her name. As if in reply to his silent plea, she looked up. Slowly, so slowly she lifted her face to his—a face as pale as parchment, eyes whose luminescence rivaled that of the moonglow. He gasped at that face which haunted his dreams.

Elise.

She seemed as surprised as he was. She stood, the book falling to the floor of the gazebo, a flutter of pages that made no sound when it hit. Her image rippled, as if reflected off the surface of the pond.

Elise!

He started to run, knowing that even if he reached her it would be like trying to hold moonlight in his arms. Her image wavered, shifting in and out of substance as he drew closer, becoming moonbeams and shadows and silver haze. When he reached the gazebo, she was gone. Only her essence remained, a mist of memory. He was alone, wondering why she'd come again only to leave him as mysteriously as she'd appeared.

He turned, searching the woods for a sign of her, nearly tripping when his foot bumped against the book that had fallen from her lap. He reached down and picked it up, afraid it would evaporate the moment he touched it, but it remained solid.

The binding was warm, as if holding onto the imprint of her hand. He clasped it to his chest, trying to hold back the flood of emotions threatening to overwhelm him in misery.

He knew why Elise had come to him. She'd come to remind him of his promise, a promise he'd almost broken.

"I'm sorry," he whispered, but his words were absorbed by the night.

He opened the book. There was no title, no author, no introduction. Every page was blank. Every page except the last.

On the final page were written the words, "The End."

CHAPTER ELEVEN

"You look like hell," Herb said when Robert came to the garage.

Robert pulled up a chair and took the Coke his friend offered. "Thanks. I didn't get much sleep last night." He'd already convinced himself last night's vision had been nothing more than a dream. This morning there had been no sign of the book that had felt so solid in his hands the night before. Just a dream.

It had seemed so real, though. He'd passed the gazebo on the way into town. It had looked bright and cheery in the morning sunlight. The thought of it being haunted was laughable. There were no signs of ghostly visitations. No sign that Elise had been there.

He shook the image away and turned to his friend. "Did you see Liz?"

"We had dinner with her last night," Herb said. "Charming lady. Janie and I have decided she's too good for you."

Robert disguised his snort by taking a long swig of the soft drink while Herb sorted through a cluttered drawer for the keys to the Jeep.

"Is she still in town?" Robert asked, trying to sound casual.

"She'd better be. Her car's here." Herb explained about the muffler, telling Robert he expected to have it replaced within a day or so.

Robert wasn't sure whether to be relieved or not. That could explain why she hadn't come back to the cottage. Or it could be the only reason she hadn't already left town. The question was, should he let her go or beg her to stay? Maybe the dream was a subconscious warning to keep his distance before he allowed his guilty yearnings to break the vow he'd made to his wife. Or maybe he was just going crazy.

"You could stop over to Stone Haven," Herb said. "She said she'd be staying there until the car was fixed."

Robert nodded and took his keys.

"Are we on for dinner and chess tonight?" Herb asked as Robert turned to leave. "Janie's making apple pies. Maybe you could take home a few."

Robert chuckled. "Knowing Janie, that would still leave you with enough pies to open a small bake shop."

Herb patted his ample middle and smiled. "What can I say? I love the woman, despite her faults."

"You're a lucky man," Robert said, opening the door. As the bell tinkled overhead, he heard Herb give a soft grunt of agreement. *What I wouldn't give to have what you have*, Robert thought.

Outside he stood on the sidewalk, looking down the street in the direction of the bed and breakfast. There was no sign of Liz. Even if there was, he still wouldn't have moved.

It would have been enough just to look at her.

* * *

Liz couldn't stand being cooped up inside for another minute. Her room at Stone Haven, which had seemed charming at first, now felt suffocating and unbearably lonely. The face staring back at her from the mirror seemed to belong to someone else, almost as if she'd left her real self—her true self—back at the cottage. These last few days had been like a fairy tale, but unlike Sleeping Beauty, she'd awakened only to find the years had slipped away, stripping her of her youth and beauty.

Only this time, instead of the slow, gradual process of aging over years, it had happened overnight. Now she saw things she hadn't noticed before—the tiny vertical lines when she pursed her lips, the thinning of her upper lip, which had always been full and pouty. Her hair seemed thinner, her eyes were paler, duller, and the skin around them puffier. Or maybe she was simply over-obsessing.

She'd undressed in the dark last night rather than come face to face with the naked ravages of time. Some time during the night she'd thought she'd heard Robert calling her name, but it had only been a dream.

She thought she'd hear from him today. He knew she was here. Maybe he was waiting for her to call him. Or maybe he was glad she was gone and he didn't have to follow behind her in the cottage, putting everything back where it belonged.

She decided to go out and explore Coldwater Springs. Hadn't that been the reason for this trip in the first place? She'd wanted to see the country. Not only the historic and tourist sites, but the hidden, out-of-the-way treasures along the back roads and small towns. Well, that's exactly what she'd do.

But what if she ran into Robert? She wavered for a moment, unsure whether she wanted to risk bumping into him outside the magical walls of the cottage. It was either that or become a hermit for the duration of her stay in

Coldwater Springs. She decided to take the chance and stepped outside.

While she stood on the sidewalk trying to decide which direction to walk, someone called out her name. She turned and saw Janie waving.

"Hi," Janie said, reaching her. "I thought I'd stop by and see if you wanted to join me for lunch."

"I'd love that," Liz said, grateful for the company. She already felt the stirrings of friendship forming. Janie was comfortable to talk to and pleasant company. As they walked, Janie pointed out homes on the historic registry, sprinkling the sightseeing tour with local gossip.

Janie led her down a side street to a small café where they were seated at a corner booth. Looking up from the menu, Liz caught Janie staring intently at the cameo brooch on her blouse.

"That's a beautiful brooch," Janie said. "Where did you get it?"

"Actually," Liz replied, "This brooch is the reason I'm here to begin with." She told Janie about her stop at the antique store that had led to getting lost in the storm and ending up on Robert's doorstep.

She felt a fluttering in her chest just thinking of him. It was a moment before she realized Janie was staring at her. *Oh God*, she thought. *Have I given myself away?*

"He was a perfect gentleman," she stuttered, trying to mask the emotions that must have shown on her face. Why else would Janie be looking at her so disapprovingly? What must she be thinking?

Janie pointed to the brooch. "It just looks so familiar. Could I see it?"

Liz nodded and unpinned the brooch, handing it to Janie and watching as she turned it over, a frown on her face.

"If the phones had been working I would have called a garage right then," Liz explained. "But the power was out and we couldn't call and it was raining so hard." She had a feeling it sounded like a poor excuse.

Janie didn't seem to be listening. She handed the brooch back, her lips pursed, then changed the subject.

The rest of the lunch was filled with small talk, but something had changed. They acted normal, but Liz felt as though Janie was watching her, gauging her actions. With a sinking feeling, Liz realized Janie must suspect her stay at the cottage wasn't as innocent as it sounded.

When Liz made an excuse to call it a day, Janie didn't argue. There was no invitation for dinner that night, either.

* * *

Liz returned to Stone Haven feeling ashamed and confused. Janie's turnaround from friendly companionship to suspicious disapproval only reinforced her belief that society would shun her for carrying on with a man half her age. People might not say anything to their faces, but there would be snickers behind their backs and nasty, malicious gossip. She was halfway up the stairs when the desk person called her back.

"Ms. Riley? I have a message here for you," she said, digging through a pile of papers on her desk.

Liz felt her heartbeat quicken. A message! Her first thought was that Robert had called after all. She waited impatiently while the woman shuffled slips of paper, finally finding what she was looking for. When Liz read the message her heart sank. It wasn't from Robert.

She thanked the woman and returned to her room. She should have expected it, should have known her real life would intrude. She dialed the number and prepared herself for the lecture she knew was coming when her son answered the phone.

"Mom, what are you still doing in Colorado? I thought you'd be halfway home by now."

"Oh, I had a little problem with the car." She glossed over the details, not wanting to give Teddy any reason to say *I told you so*. "Nothing to worry about. It's in the garage being taken care of right now."

"Keep an eye on those mechanics," he said. "I watched a news program about how they rip off unsuspecting travelers. Make sure you ask for any parts they take out and don't let them cheat you."

Liz sighed. Teddy took his role as man of the house seriously. She had to remind him she was an adult and capable of venturing out in the big bad world on her own. "I'm fine, Teddy. Did Marcie give you this number? How's the baby?"

Teddy's voice grew somber. "That's why I called."

Liz gripped the phone, her heart thudding. "What's wrong?"

"The baby's fine," Teddy assured her quickly. "It's Marcie I'm worried about. She's pretty run down. I just want to be sure I know where to reach you at all times. Just in case."

She didn't want to think of what "just in case" might mean.

"Will you be heading home soon?" he asked.

Yes, Liz thought. Just as soon as I'm done with this crazy, reckless love affair with a man half my age. Wouldn't that freak Teddy out. He'd have her locked up for sure. She felt the crushing weight of responsibility like a shroud.

"There's no rush," she said. "I may extend my vacation a little since I don't have to be back to work until September." That was as much as she was willing to admit for now—even to herself.

When she hung up, her hands shook. She chided herself for being so selfish when her family needed her. Without actually saying it, Teddy had come close to implying she was going through a mid-life crisis. Could that be it? Is that why she had convinced herself she'd found the fountain of youth?

She was overcome with guilt. This was a stupid plan. As soon as her car was repaired she was heading home where she belonged. She'd leave Robert a note, thanking him for his hospitality, and never look back.

She had to go home. She had to leave Robert, even if it tore her heart out.

* * *

Janie placed a second piece of apple pie on Robert's plate and sat across from him. "I had lunch with Liz today," she said.

At the sound of her name he caught his breath. He realized he'd been waiting all night for someone to mention her. He'd even half expected to find her here tonight. Janie and Herb were two of the most caring people in all of Colorado and he knew they'd taken a shine to Liz. "How is she?" he asked.

Janie frowned. "She seems fine. But Robert, I have to tell you something..."

He waited while Janie chewed on her bottom lip, as if

trying to find the best way to say whatever was on her mind. "Janie?"

She sighed and looked up at him with an apologetic expression. "I really liked her," she said finally. "But I think she's a thief."

"What?" That was the last thing he expected. "A thief? Why in the world would you think that?"

Janie reached out and put her hand over his. "Robert, she was wearing Elise's brooch. The one her grandmother left her. She said she bought it at an antique store, but she was right there in your home..." Janie shook her head as if it was too painful to finish, then rushed on. "I looked at the back of the brooch. I read the inscription. There's no doubt in my mind it was Elise's cameo."

Robert remembered the inscription on the back of the brooch. One word—*Hope*. That had been Elise's grandmother's name. Hope. The inscription, however, had always seemed to represent more, so much more. He'd lost both the brooch and its promise of hope when Elise died.

"Janie," he said, closing his hand around hers. "Thank you for telling me, but that brooch has been missing for longer than I can remember. I searched for it for years. That and Elise's wedding ring. I never found either one."

"But Robert, she was right there in Elise's room. She could have found it someplace you'd overlooked."

He smiled. "I searched every inch of the cottage. I didn't overlook anything. Besides, I know beyond a shadow of a doubt that Liz would never have stolen it if I had."

Janie took a long, deep sigh. "Thank God. I didn't

want to believe it either, but when I saw the cameo and the inscription..." She squeezed his hand. "You're right. Liz wouldn't have stolen it. But it *is* Elise's brooch. How did it turn up at the antique store to begin with?"

Robert shook his head, wondering the same thing. "I don't know."

"Well, why don't you just call the antique store and find out?" Herb piped up.

They both looked at him, as if surprised to find him there.

"Of course," Janie cried, jumping up. They'll still be open." She handed Robert the telephone while she flipped through the phone book, then recited the number while he dialed.

When he explained why he was calling, the clerk perked up. She remembered the brooch and the customer both. "Oh, she fell in love with the brooch the moment she saw it. When she turned it over and read the inscription her eyes just lit up and she said it was the perfect prayer to wear close to her heart."

Robert smiled. That sounded so much like Liz. He could almost see the wistful look on her face as she read it, her lips moving soundlessly as she repeated the word. "Could you tell me where you got the brooch in the first place?" he asked.

"Well," the clerk replied. "That's the strangest part. I'd never seen it before. I was rearranging the jewelry display and noticed it for the first time. I picked it up to look at it the very moment the customer walked in the door." There was a soft laugh at the other end of the line. "I thought it seemed like a perfect case of synchronicity."

"I agree," Robert said.

Or destiny, he added silently.

CHAPTER TWELVE

That night, Robert paced the empty rooms of the cottage, struggling with his emotions. He felt torn between his loyalty to his wife and his growing feelings for Liz.

When he'd jumped to Liz's defense earlier, the response was automatic and unquestionable. He may only have known her a few days, but there was no doubt in his mind as to her character and honesty. In the short time he'd known her, she'd managed to melt some of the ice around his heart. It was both a blessing and a curse, for now he craved the warmth she'd shown him. That yearning, he was sure, explained last night's dream. But was Elise's vision a reminder or a warning?

He heard a familiar scratching and opened the door. Tallulah waddled in. "Well," he said. "Does this mean you're not mad at me anymore?" He took her acceptance of a square of chocolate to be a yes. Instead of curling on his lap after her treat, Tallulah walked away, nudged open the door to Elise's room, and disappeared inside.

He followed, pushing the door all the way open. Since he'd moved into the spare bedroom, he thought of this as Elise's room, but it was the room they'd shared together as man and wife. It was where they'd made love and where she'd sent her last breath to heaven. Everything was exactly the way she'd left it, down to the smallest detail.

As always, the first sight of Elise's room tugged at his heart, bringing with it a torrent of bittersweet memories. He could almost see her there, brushing her hair in front of the mirror or reading in the rocking chair beside the bed. Now Liz's presence shared a space here, too. He remembered the shock of seeing her before the mirror, twin images of beauty and grace. How she'd trembled when he'd covered her nakedness with his shirt. He'd wanted her so badly. The desire had been so sudden and unexpected it had nearly brought him to his knees. He hadn't felt that way since Elise and he never thought he would again. But that was before Liz had stepped in out of the rain and entered his life.

He spotted Tallulah curled up on the terrycloth slippers Liz had left behind. A few days ago he would have picked them up and moved them out of the room, leaving Elise's shrine undisturbed. Tonight he only found himself wondering if Liz's feet were cold.

"You miss her, don't you Tallulah?"

The raccoon just stared at him with dark, soulful eyes.

"So do I," he sighed. "So do I."

He walked over and touched the pillow, gently running the back of his curled fingers along the indentation where her head had rested. It seemed warm to his touch, as if she'd just lifted her head from the pillow. He lay down and settled his head in the same spot, closing his eyes. The faintest trace of her perfume lingered, an intoxicating blend of almond and vanilla. His body relaxed and the peace he'd been seeking all night found him.

It was the cold which finally awakened him. He

shivered and reached blindly for the blanket. Something soft brushed past his cheek, then he heard a scrabbling at the window. He opened his eyes, disoriented and surprised to find himself in Elise's room. The temperature in the room plummeted. Tallulah scratched and clawed at the window, her fur bristling. She turned and hissed, staring into the darkened room.

Robert reached over, flipped the latch, and let the agitated animal out, his eyes growing accustomed to the dark. There were layers to the darkness, textures upon textures of black and charcoal and ebony, swirling and merging around a pinpoint of midnight blue. The blue flame flickered and danced, alone at first, then joined by another light swaying to the same celestial music.

Suddenly he was assaulted by the scent of roses, a scent which reminded him of Elise. Mesmerized by the dreamy play of light, Robert sat up and watched the twin glows expand, spreading their gentle radiance into the darkness, taking shape until the pale center became the glowing form of a woman. He realized the twin was simply the reflection of the dancing light in the cheval mirror.

The shimmering ice-blue form closest had her back to him, naked and luminescent against the velvety darkness. The mirror-image reflection took on substance, a face eerily familiar. He was struck by a sense of deja vu as the image took shape. It was Liz's face he saw in the mirror, looking the way she had the morning he'd glimpsed her through the open doorway.

"Liz?" His voice was absorbed by the dense darkness. Slowly the form closest began to turn. Its mirror image never moved, however, adding to the surreal quality of the vision. Robert gasped as the apparition turned to face him. But instead of Liz, this time it was Elise's face that stared at him. He gasped, looking from one ghostly specter to the other. Elise. Liz. Then back to Elise, who held up a finger to her lips, compelling him to watch without interruption.

He wanted to scream, to cry out and dispel the image, shatter it into shrieking, glittering shards. But he couldn't move. The numbing cold paralyzed him and the scene which played out before his eyes held him spellbound. A strangled moan escaped his trembling lips.

He focused on the one seemingly solid image in the unearthly tableau—a shimmering band on Elise's finger. Her wedding ring. The ring he'd never found encircled her finger.

Elise nodded, as if he'd caught an important clue. She reached out and twisted the ring off her finger, slowly sliding it up and over her knuckle, off the tip of her finger, then holding it out as if offering the ring to Robert. An ethereal glow shimmered from the gold band, sending a corona of rays outward and dispelling the cold blue light with a golden warmth.

He shook his head. *No. I won't take it back*, he screamed silently. *Don't make me.*

Elise turned the ring three times, filling the room with brilliance, then held it still. She smiled at him the way a teacher smiles at a bright student struggling over a problem. Patiently. Leaning forward a bit as if willing him to figure it out by the power of her belief.

Then she turned back to the mirror, her back to him. She reached out, holding the ring toward the mirror. The surface of the mirror shimmered and blurred. Her hand touched it, palm skimming along the surface, then dipping, sending ripples outward before disappearing beneath the surface, as if dipping through a sheer waterfall.

At the same time the reflection of Liz on the other side reached forward, meeting Elise's outstretched hand. Beneath the mirrored surface, Liz's hand closed around the ring and cradled it within her palm, accepting the gift. For a moment the two hands joined, then parted. Liz's hand cupped around the ring while Elise's retreated back through the glass, empty.

She turned back to Robert. Her lips pursed and he knew she was going to speak. He shook his head, not wanting to hear what she would say.

"Robert."

The sound of her voice sent rolling waves of grief through him. How could he have forgotten her voice? Hearing it again tugged at his soul. "Oh, Elise," he moaned.

"Shh," she murmured. "Promise me..."

"Yes," he cried. "Yes." He wouldn't forget his promise again. That's why she was here, to remind him. He would promise her anything, over and over beyond eternity. Anything she wanted. This time he'd be strong.

Before he could beg her forgiveness for almost breaking his promise, she stopped him, her voice trembling. "Promise me you'll love again, Robert. Promise you'll be happy and bring love back to our enchanted cottage." The words came in a torrent before he could question or argue. Her image blurred, as if the effort of speaking sapped whatever strength held him together.

"Promise me," she begged, her eyes pinning him.

"Elise?"

"Promise," she pleaded, stepping backward. At the

same time the mirror image stepped forward and Robert watched as the two images blended and merged into one woman, arms held out beseechingly. The image faded from Elise to Liz, then settling finally into Elise again.

He jerked forward, breaking free of the paralysis as the image faded. His heart pounded and sweat beaded his forehead as he called out her name. "Elise!"

As quickly as it had appeared, the vision faded to a speck of blue brilliance before flickering out completely in the encroaching darkness. As Elise left him again he finally realized the promise she'd tried to extract all those years ago. He'd misunderstood her meaning all along.

She was gone, leaving only darkness behind. Darkness, but not emptiness. She'd freed him from a life of loneliness by releasing him from his misguided vow.

A gentle breeze drifted through the room, sighing in a soft lament. "Let go, Robert. You have to let me go now."

He shivered, remembering Liz murmuring those exact words in her sleep. How long had Elise been trying to reach him? Had she really been here or was it simply a dream? Had he been keeping a promise which shackled her spirit to earth instead of freeing her?

Now Elise's spirit had returned, releasing him from his vow and freeing him to love again. She was right, he realized. It was time to move on. Time to love again. He'd been alone too long.

As the first oblique rays of the rising sun brightened the window, he reached for the phone.

* * *

Liz jumped up and reached for the phone, answering

on the first ring before she was fully awake.

"Liz, I need you."

"What?" She ran her fingers through her hair. "Robert?"

"Please," he begged. "I need to talk to you. Can I come over?"

She sat up, pulling the blankets up with her. Even through her sleep-fogged brain she realized she couldn't let him see her here. "No!" she cried. "I mean...I'll come to the cottage."

"But your car—"

"Herb gave me a loaner," she explained. "He insisted I take the car—and a pie. I can be there in an hour." As she rubbed the sleep from her eyes, she wondered why he'd called her so early. And why now? She hadn't heard a word from him all day yesterday. "Robert, are you all right?"

There was an undercurrent of desperation in his voice. "All right or all wrong, I don't know which. I just know I need to talk to you. Please?"

She couldn't have said no even if she'd listened to the warning voices in her head. She needed him as much as he seemed to need her. She couldn't resist—even if it was only one final day before returning to her real world. One final day as a young woman with dreams and visions. One final day to be loved before moving on to the next phase of her life.

"Yes," she said. "Yes. I'll be there."

CHAPTER THIRTEEN

Liz took a quick shower, dressed, and was on her way out the door in only half an hour. She threw some things into a small overnight bag—just in case. There was a lightness to her step and a secret smile on her face as she swept past the registration desk, almost knocking over Janie Hepplewhite in her rush to her car.

"Liz," Janie cried, reaching for her arm. "I was just on my way up to see you."

Oh, not now, Liz thought. She wanted to reach Robert before she had a chance to change her mind.

Janie caught her glancing at her watch. "It'll only take a minute," she said. "Please?"

Liz didn't want to hurt the woman's feelings. Janie and Herb had been so kind to her. The least she could do was give her a moment of her time. "Of course," she said. "Why don't we talk over coffee?"

Janie looked relieved as they made their way to the dining room, where Amanda was setting out a tray of assorted pastries alongside the coffee carafe. She nodded to both women and called Janie by name. Liz was reminded again of what a small town Coldwater Springs was. She remembered Janie's comment that everyone knew everyone else. How many people already knew she'd spent the night at Robert's cottage? Who might suspect she was on her way there right now? She'd probably already destroyed his reputation in this town. Now Janie wanted to speak with her. Why? To warn her away from him?

Janie stared into her coffee, not meeting her gaze. The spoon clinked against the curved edges of the thick ceramic cup as she stirred her coffee over and over...and over. It was obvious she was working up the courage to say something and Liz wasn't sure she wanted to hear it. She was about ready to scream with annoyance when Janie stopped stirring, took a deep breath and looked her in the eye.

"I owe you an apology," Janie explained. "I jumped to the wrong conclusion about something and misjudged you."

The statement took Liz totally by surprise. "I don't understand," she muttered. She waited while Janie stammered over her reply.

"Yesterday when we were at lunch and I saw the brooch you were wearing, it was such a shock." Janie wrung her hands, forcing each word out. "Elise had one just like it."

At first Liz didn't understand, but slowly what Janie was saying started to fall into place.

"Her grandmother's name was inscribed on the back of the brooch," Janie explained.

"Hope?" Liz asked, afraid of the answer, but knowing she was right.

Janie nodded.

It all made sense to Liz now. The sudden coolness she'd felt at lunch yesterday, the way Janie had studied the brooch, then gone quiet. She reached for Janie's hand. "You thought I stole it from Robert?"

Again Janie nodded, slowly, her eyes glistening. "I'm

sorry. I didn't want to believe it, but—"

Liz stopped her, realizing how it must have looked. A stranger comes into town, spends the night at a friend's house and suddenly shows up wearing his dead wife's jewelry. "I understand," she said, squeezing Janie's hand. "I would have wondered the same thing. Robert and Elise were good friends, and you didn't really know me that well."

"That's not true," Janie argued. "I may not have known you long, but I knew you weren't someone I had to hide the good silver from." She frowned and shook her head. "It's just that I'd seen Elise wearing that brooch so many times. I know how much it meant to her." She blinked tears from her eyes. "Seeing it again was such a shock." She dropped her gaze. "I'm sorry."

Liz took the brooch off. Its beauty was tarnished now and she felt guilty wearing it. More than that, she regretted the discomfort it had forced between herself and Janie.

"I really do understand," Liz said. "Please don't be upset."

Janie looked up, her lips pressed into a tight smile, as if she didn't deserve forgiveness.

A sudden suspicion sent a chill through Liz. Janie must have told Robert. Is that why he wanted to see her this morning? She tried to imagine what his reaction might have been. Shock? Betrayal? Disappointment? What must he think of her?

"Janie," she said, her voice trembling. "Does Robert think I stole this from him?"

"Oh no!" Janie cried out, her eyes wide. "He told me it was ridiculous to even think such a thing and said he knew beyond a doubt that you were incapable of stealing from him or anyone else. Besides, he said the brooch had been missing for as long as he could remember."

Although relieved to know Robert didn't blame her, Liz felt an intense need to clear her name once and for all. There was no question the sudden appearance of the brooch now, after she'd spent so much time alone in the cottage, was suspicious. Maybe Robert believed her, and perhaps Janie regretted initially suspecting her, but would other people be so willing to trust her?

"I have to get to the bottom of this," Liz said. "I'm going out to that antique store."

Janie stopped her. "Don't bother," she said. "They have no idea where the brooch came from or when it showed up. All I can think of is that Elise lost it and somehow it found its way to the antique store. There's no other explanation."

Liz frowned. There had to be an explanation, and until she found it, there'd always be a shroud of doubt surrounding her. She wanted to clear her name.

The sounds of clattering silverware and voices raised in conversation filled the dining room as more guests arrived for breakfast. Liz traced her finger across the engraved backing of the cameo. *Hope*. It seemed more than a name. It seemed like a prophecy, a message directed solely at her.

"Janie," Liz asked, her voice soft with yearning. "Are you happy?"

"Happy?" Janie seemed to taste the word, to roll it around her mouth and test its boundaries. "I'm content."

"I don't think that's the same," Liz replied. "Do you ever feel empty? Unfulfilled?"

When Janie shook her head slowly, Liz continued. "For so many years I defined myself as a wife and mother. Now my kids are grown and my husband is gone. I don't know who I am anymore."

When Janie clasped her hand, the simple gesture was enough to bring tears to her eyes. "I'm sorry," Liz said with an embarrassed laugh. "I'm having an attack of hormones."

"Or loneliness," Janie replied.

Liz nodded. "I guess I never realized how lonely I was until I saw that same emptiness in Robert's eyes. It's as if when Elise died he lost the will to go forward. The cottage is a shrine to her memory."

Janie frowned. "He's talked to you about Elise?"

"Yes. Why?"

"It's just that he never mentions her. Never speaks her name, as if it's still too painful to say." Janie stirred her coffee, struggling to find the right words. "I always felt if he would only talk about her it wouldn't hurt so much."

"Maybe he's ready now. Maybe he's decided to stop hurting."

"Or maybe you found a way behind that wall he erected. Maybe you were able to do something we couldn't do—give him a reason to want to live again."

Liz refused to take the credit. "It's easier to talk to strangers when the pain goes that deep."

"I don't think Robert thinks of you as a stranger, Liz."

She searched Janie's eyes for signs of disapproval. Surely she must suspect those feelings went both ways. Yet Janie never batted an eye. If she found it odd, she didn't say.

Liz checked her watch. She was already late, but knew she couldn't go to the cottage until her questions about the brooch were answered. She tucked the brooch into her pocket and reached for her purse.

"You're going to the antique store, aren't you?" Janie asked.

"Yes. I have to." It wouldn't take long and she knew she wouldn't be comfortable seeing Robert until she had some answers herself.

Janie nodded and after a brief hug goodbye, Liz wound her way through the dining room. It had filled up since they'd entered and she could feel people watching her, pointing and whispering. Maybe she was being paranoid, but she couldn't help wondering just how much gossip about her and Robert had already made its way through the small town.

* * *

First Robert paced, then he worried. Then he paced some more. Where was Liz? She said she'd be right over. Had she changed her mind? He didn't want to think about other possibilities. If anything happened to her...

Stop it, he chided himself. *She's fine.* It just seemed as if it was taking forever because he couldn't wait to talk to her. He wanted to tell her about his dream and what he thought it meant and whether she thought it meant the same thing.

Bursting with nervous energy, he began moving furniture. A little at first, but then when he didn't feel the usual apprehension seeing things out of place, he went at it with a growing sense of release. He moved the rocking chair in front of the fireplace and shoved the love seat back against the wall. He rearranged the end tables and lamps, then stepped back and surveyed the changes. The room looked different. Bigger. But it didn't feel wrong.

That's when he knew for sure that Elise had released him from his deathbed promise. Either that or he had released himself to move on without feeling he was betraying her memory. Either way, he realized that Elise would have wanted that, even if she hadn't been able to speak the words. She would never have expected he'd bury himself alive beside her.

He thought he heard a car outside and stepped to the front door. It wasn't Liz, however. As always, the view from his front door calmed him. He loved the mountains. Their gentle slopes, lush curves and secret valleys reminded him of a woman's body, ripe with promise. He wanted to share this view, as well as his heart and his life. He was ready to live again, ready to move on and let go of the past.

If only Liz would come back.

* * *

Instead of driving to the cottage, Liz went directly to the antique store. There she heard exactly the same thing Janie had told her. There was no record of where or when they'd acquired the cameo, and no one remembered seeing it before she walked in that day and bought it. The clerk apologized for the oversight, telling her they kept very good records, but somehow this one item had slipped through the cracks. She assured Liz that if she was unhappy with the purchase she could return it. Liz shook her head. She'd return it, but not to the antique store. She'd return it to its rightful owner—Robert.

She checked her watch. She'd told Robert she'd be there hours ago. Maybe he thought she'd changed her mind. She'd spent the morning on a wild goose chase. The visit to the antique store had only raised more questions. She drove slowly to the cottage. Why had she wasted her time running around all morning when Janie had told her they didn't know where the brooch came from?

As she pulled into the cottage driveway, she realized exactly what she'd been doing. She'd been avoiding this moment. Because she knew as soon as she walked through that door she would be making a commitment that would change her life.

She took a deep breath, her mind a jumble of emotions—fear, excitement, anticipation and worry. She wanted to go through that door and never look back. The appeal of recapturing her youth and finding love again was so seductive. But at what risk? The opposite pull was just as strong. She prided herself on being dependable and loyal, not only to her family, but her community. Her life had followed the predictable path laid out for her and she'd never complained, never yearned for more.

From the corner of her eye she saw the door of the cottage open. She looked up to see Robert standing there, leaning against the door jamb. Waiting.

Her hands trembled. She couldn't move forward and couldn't retreat. He just stood there, waiting so patiently for her to decide. All she had to do was make a choice— one way or the other.

She reached into her pocket and pulled out the brooch. She wouldn't leave without returning it to him. That much she knew. She turned the brooch, running her finger over the single word etched into the gold backing. *Hope.* Was that the appeal? Had she lost the ability to hope? Maybe what Robert was offering was the chance to dream again, something she'd almost forgotten how to do. Maybe it was something he needed as desperately as she did. If she turned her back on him, she'd never know. If she left now, she'd regret it the rest of her life.

She took a deep breath, straightened her shoulders, and slipped the brooch back into her pocket. As she withdrew her hand, the missing age spot confirmed that the magic of the cottage wasn't an illusion, but that didn't matter. When she opened the door and walked up the path toward Robert, it wasn't her youth she was choosing.

She was choosing love.

When Liz stepped out of the car, Robert felt the tension drain from his body. He released a breath and forced himself to relax. He'd been so afraid she'd leave without giving him a chance. The thought of never seeing her again had filled him with dread.

She moved slowly, hesitantly. He stood perfectly still, afraid any movement would spook her and send her running back to the car. He could read the turmoil in her eyes and it tugged at his heart. Slowly, without realizing it, his hand came up, palm extended toward her.

Her step quickened as she closed the distance between them. He pushed away from the doorway, taking one step closer and holding out his arms. She began running, tears streaming from her eyes as she rushed into his arms, as if finally realizing how much he wanted and needed her there, and knowing she needed exactly the same thing.

He crushed her to his chest, lifting her off her feet and pulling her close. He buried his face in her hair, holding her in the shelter of his arms. Neither spoke.

Neither moved.

As they swayed, locked together on the threshold of the enchanted cottage, time forever stood still.

CHAPTER FOURTEEN

Liz wasn't sure where the tears came from. It was as if a torrent of emotion she'd held barricaded inside had suddenly been set loose, flooding through her with a roaring, rushing release. She'd run to him as if she'd spent her whole life searching for this one moment in time. When his arms closed around her, she knew she'd made the only choice possible. Nothing had ever felt so right.

Robert carried her inside, crooning and murmuring her fears away. He sat on the rocker, cradling her to his chest and pushing off with one foot, rocking her slow and gentle.

"Shhh," he said as her sobs dwindled to sighs. She knew there'd be time for words later. Right now all she wanted was to lose herself in the soothing rhythm as they rocked together in the quiet enchantment of the cottage.

Time played tricks on her here. When they were together time seemed to fly, and when they were apart it dragged interminably. It could have been moments or hours later when she finally noticed the changes in the room.

"Robert?" She looked up into his face. "Things are different."

"Yes," he replied, smiling. "Things are different."

"I mean the room," she said. "You've changed everything around."

"Do you like it?"

Like it? She couldn't believe her eyes. The other day he'd nearly tripped over himself putting the sugar bowl back where it belonged. Today everything was out of place.

He brushed the hair back from her forehead and explained. "I had a dream, or a vision, or something." He frowned, then went on. "I realized that Elise wouldn't want me to turn the cottage into a shrine. She wouldn't want me to spend the rest of my life mourning her."

What was he saying? Liz only nodded, not wanting to interrupt as he told her about the strange dream he'd had. Was it a dream? The way he told her it was almost as if he believed Elise's ghost had come to send him a message. When he repeated the words she'd left him with, Liz felt a chill ripple along her spine. She remembered saying those same exact words to him only a few nights ago—words she'd thought were leftover fragments of a dream. "*Let me go,*" she'd said. "*You have to let me go.*"

"Don't you see?" Robert explained. "I wasn't honoring Elise's memory by keeping everything the same. I was tying her to this earth. Her spirit wanted to be set free, but I wouldn't let go."

Liz didn't know what to think. She certainly didn't believe in ghosts. But she didn't believe in a fountain of youth either, and here she was—young again. Besides, there was a certain logic to his explanation. Whatever the reason, it was obvious that something had given Robert a reason to hope again.

Hope! That reminded her. "Robert," she said, scrambling in her pocket for the brooch. "Janie told me about the brooch. That's why I was late."

"Oh Liz, I never thought—"

"I know," she said, stopping him. "Thank you for believing in me." She shook her head. "It's so strange. I went to the antique store, but they had no record of where it came from. No one had ever seen it before I showed up that day." She looked up at him, pleading for an answer neither had. "Why now? Why me?"

"I don't know. Maybe it's destiny."

The word hung in the air between them. *Destiny*. It didn't make sense, but what did? Since she'd arrived dripping wet on his doorstep, nothing about this ripple in time made any sense—not the effect the cottage had on her body, nor the effect Robert had on her heart and soul. She was tired of trying to force logic onto a preposterous situation.

She tried to give the brooch to Robert, but he wouldn't take it. "It belongs to you," she said, forcing it into his hand.

"No. It belongs to you," he argued. Carefully he pinned it to her blouse. "It led you to me. It's a sign that there's still hope for both of us. If you ever forget that, just read the inscription on the back. *Hope*. It's more than a name, it's a choice."

Do you believe in magic? Do you believe in destiny? "Yes," she said, resting her head on his shoulder and letting him rock all further questions away.

Liz wouldn't let any lingering doubts ruin their time together. She pushed all concerns out of her mind and surrendered willingly.

Robert brushed a stray curl from her forehead. "You're so beautiful," he said, a tenderness to his voice that sent a shiver rippling through her body.

She didn't argue. She knew he didn't see her the way

she really was, but it didn't matter. Maybe she was only beautiful right here and right now, but Robert made her believe it was true—at least in his eyes. It had nothing to do with the enchantment of the cottage. He saw her through the eyes of love, the most powerful magic of all.

Holding her gaze, he cupped her cheek and brushed his thumb slowly across her lips, making them tingle with desire.

"Robert," she whispered. "There are things you don't know about me."

He leaned forward, touching his lips to hers so tenderly, then moving away. "I know everything I need to know," he said. "I know you've always colored within the lines, doing everything the way you thought it should be done."

He kissed her again, longer this time. "I know you always put your own needs last, taking care of everyone else even when it means denying yourself."

And again. "I know you think too much, when you should be feeling."

This time he didn't break the kiss and she didn't want him to. She felt things she hadn't felt in a long time, feelings she thought she'd forgotten. He was right. Just this once she wanted to color outside the lines, to put her own needs first, to stop thinking and let herself feel and accept everything he had to offer.

She wrapped her arms around his neck, pulling him close and losing herself in the delicious ripeness of his lips. His breath was a warm caress that met hers and merged so that when she inhaled she seemed to accept him into her very soul. With gentle insistence he parted her lips and she welcomed his tentative probing with a wild abandon, barely aware when he lifted and carried her into his room and laid her on the bed. The mattress dipped as he lowered himself beside her. "I love you, Liz," he murmured. "I love you and need you in my life."

She turned toward him, seeking his warmth the way a flower bends to the sunlight. She fitted her body to his, stretching and lengthening along every hard curve and dip of his lean frame, marveling at how perfectly they fit together.

He raised himself on his elbow and held her gaze. "Tell me you love me too," he said.

She reached for him, but he stopped her, covering her hand with his. "Don't think," he cautioned. "Just feel. Tell me what's in your heart. Nothing else matters."

With just those words, the final barrier crumbled. "I love you," she said, softly at first as she tested the words on her lips, then with a growing passion and belief. Now that she'd admitted it to herself, she couldn't stop the words from overflowing. "I love you. I love you. I love you. Nothing else matters."

His answer was a low growl as he lowered himself over her, his kisses hungrier, more demanding. She met his insistence with a rising passion that surprised her. In a rush, she tore at his shirt, running her hands across his bare chest, then burying her face against his neck, tasting the salty maleness of his skin, feeling his pulse pounding against her lips.

He moaned and arched his hips, grinding his weight against her until she thought she'd scream with the need to have him, to hold him deep inside her and feel their bodies joined the way they were destined to be.

Her whispered declarations of love became an entreaty. "Love me," she pleaded.

"I do, I do," he murmured, leaving a trail of hot

kisses along her skin as he undressed her. Neither of them needed any further urging as the momentum carried them away. When he entered her she felt as if she held within her body the answer to every one of life's mysteries.

They made love slowly, savoring every exquisite moment, each new sensation. He brought her to the brink of surrender, holding her body and her gaze, then releasing her with a whispered promise as he took her deeper than she'd ever been before.

Afterward he cradled her in his arms, making her feel cherished beyond her wildest dreams. What moved her to tears was his assurance that neither of them would ever have to be lonely again.

* * *

Liz woke in Robert's arms, not knowing or caring how much time had passed. He was sound asleep, breathing deeply, his face tucked against her breast and one arm draped over her waist. She smiled watching him sleep, his hair mussed sexily. She brushed it away from his forehead and he sighed and nuzzled closer. She needed to get up, but didn't want to disturb him.

Remembering a trick she'd used to get sleeping babies to turn over, she brushed a fingertip across his opposite cheek. He turned his face toward her touch and curled his arms around the pillow beside him. Slowly she slid her arm from beneath his neck and climbed out of bed. She stood there a moment watching him.

Her smile turned to a thoughtful frown. If only he weren't so young. Thank God he'd been married. At least she hadn't stolen his virginity. She covered her mouth to muffle the giggle bubbling to the surface and took pride in the fact that at least she could laugh about it now. As long as she could stop herself from thinking too much, she'd be fine.

She looked around at their clothes scattered around the room. The sunlight glinted off the cameo pinned to her blouse. She didn't understand what had drawn her to the piece of jewelry and led her to Robert's doorstep. Maybe it was meant to be, like he said. Maybe it was coincidence. She didn't care. She was here now and nothing else mattered.

She reached for his shirt and slipped it on, too modest to walk across the room naked. The shirt was big on her, coming halfway down her thighs, but it would do for the quick trip to the bathroom. She walked barefoot to the doorway, running her fingers through her tousled hair. Already she missed Robert's arms around her, the pounding of his pulse against her cheek. "I'll be right back," she whispered, blowing a kiss in his direction. He mumbled a reply in his sleep which sounded like a German salutation. She smiled and padded toward the bathroom.

She never made it.

A blood-curdling screech from outside stopped her in her tracks. Her heart pounded and adrenaline rushed through her body. The cries intensified, accompanied by clawing, barking and hissing.

Liz rushed to the window just in time to see a blur of black and tan fur scurrying toward the woods. It was Tallulah and she was hurt! Liz clapped her hands and screamed "Get, get!" scaring off the stray dog that had attacked the raccoon, then ran to the door and followed the trail of scattered blood drops Tallulah left along her escape route.

CHAPTER FIFTEEN

The first thing Robert realized when he opened his eyes was that Liz was no longer in his arms. She couldn't have been gone long because the bed was still warm where her body had curled against his. The second thing he noticed was that his shirt was missing, so he simply pulled on his jeans and went searching for her.

She wasn't anywhere in the cottage. He frowned when he noticed the open door. Why would she go off into the woods alone? Then he saw the overturned planter along the path and a few drops of what looked like blood on the cobblestone path. His heart took a nosedive and an icy sheen of sweat broke out on his forehead.

"Liz!" he called. His cry echoed back to him from the hillside. "Liz, where are you?" When there was no answer, he took off running along the path leading to the gazebo, knowing without a doubt that was where she'd gone. She had to be all right. He couldn't lose her now.

He saw her up ahead, standing perfectly motionless. His heart was still pounding and he wanted to rush forward and scoop her up into his arms, but there was something about her stance, the way she was staring transfixed into the distance, that stopped him.

"Liz?" he called softly.

She didn't move.

He followed her gaze to the gazebo. His breath

caught in his throat and a flurry of goosebumps rippled along his skin. The air around him seemed denser, heavier, and he was paralyzed by a sense of *deja vu.*

Elise stood in the gazebo, morning sunlight cascading all around her. Not a dream. Not a byproduct of his imagination. The two women stood facing each other—one real and one an apparition—their gazes locked in silent communication.

Elise lifted her hand and pointed toward a rose bush alongside the gazebo. He blinked. *That couldn't be. It just couldn't be!*

Elise had sprinkled the landscape around the gazebo with roses, based not on their colors or hardiness or fragrance. She chose them by name. She'd scour catalogs, ordering only those plants with names that touched a responsive chord in her. Robert remembered her delight at finding a new plant with the perfect name. There were the English roses called *Cottage Rose*, hybrid tea roses named *Sleeping Beauty* and *Destiny*, a rose by the name of *Enchantment*, miniature roses called *Hope*, and one of her favorites—a virtually thornless old garden rose called *Maiden's Blush*.

But the roses she pointed to were her greatest disappointment—a variety named *Timeless*. Elise had jokingly referred to the plant as Time-Out, because no matter how she cared for it, the roses never bloomed.

Until today.

The plant was covered with brilliant deep rose-pink blooms as big as his fist, against dark green, semi-glossy foliage. That's where Elise's ghost pointed now—at the roses blooming where no flowers had ever bloomed before. Liz, suddenly breaking out of her trance, scrambled toward the rose bush and went down on her knees. Robert watched as Elise's spirit vanished like mist, her mission apparently accomplished. He followed Liz to the rose bush, squatting beside her.

She looked up into his eyes. "Tallulah's back here and she's hurt."

She said nothing about the vision. Robert wondered whether she'd seen anything or whether it was his own imagination, but Liz was intent on coaxing the injured raccoon out so he held his tongue. This didn't seem like the right time to ask.

Finally Liz had the raccoon on her lap. She conducted a thorough search of the squirming animal, brushing back her coat and inspecting her carefully. She turned to Robert with a puzzled frown. "She's not hurt at all. I could have sworn..."

Robert had seen the drops of blood on the cobblestones too. "Are you sure? Here, let me check." He lifted the raccoon from her arms and checked for himself. Liz was right. The animal was unhurt and waddled away, apparently tired of all the attention. "She seems fine," he said.

Liz wasn't listening. She'd turned back to the spot where Tallulah had been hiding, digging at something half buried in the dirt. She uncovered it and brushed the dirt away, holding it out to him. "Look," she said. "It's a ring."

Robert knew without even looking what it was, but he took it from her hand, holding it carefully, reverently. The inscription inside confirmed his suspicions. *Love is Timeless*, it said. "Elise's wedding ring," he whispered. "She lost it the summer before she died."

"Oh, Robert." Liz closed her hand around his tenderly. "I'm sorry."

"No," he said, seeing her through a mist of tears. "Don't you see? It's a sign."

"A sign?" Liz shook her head. "I don't—"

"Didn't you see her? In the gazebo?"

"See who?"

"Elise," he insisted. "She was standing in the gazebo pointing right to this rose bush. Then you ran here. You must have seen."

"No," Liz said. "I was following Tallulah. I thought she was hurt."

It all made such perfect sense to him. Why couldn't Liz see it? "Remember my dream?" he asked. When she nodded, he explained. "Elise passed her ring to you—this ring, the ring that's been missing for so long. And now you've found it."

"It's a coincidence."

He pushed the ring into her hand. "Read the inscription." Her lips moved. "Out loud," he said.

"Love is timeless," she read. "I still don't—"

He pointed to the rosebush. "These roses. They're called Timeless. They never bloomed before today. Is that a coincidence, too?"

Liz didn't know what to believe. He was so earnest, so intense as he listed his growing proof that Elise had sent them a mystic message.

"Another omen," he said, taking her hands in his.

She nodded slowly. Maybe it was. Or maybe he needed to believe it was. Either way, there was something different about his eyes, as if a gauzy curtain had lifted, revealing depths of emotion he'd kept hidden before. Whether real or not, Elise's vision had somehow released him from a self-imposed emotional prison.

And now, she thought, only one of them still had

reservations.

As if sensing the doubts assailing her, Robert changed the subject. He tugged on the collar of her shirt—his shirt. "I'm going to have to buy more clothes if we're going to share a wardrobe." There was a twinkle in his eye that was infectious, making her forget her earlier concerns.

"Or you could stop wearing shirts altogether," she teased, admiring the hard expanse of his bare chest.

He smiled. "I was in a hurry to find you. I was worried and you'd stolen my shirt." He ran a finger lightly along the opening at her collar. "So, what are you wearing under this?"

She blushed. "I was in a hurry too."

He curled his finger around the button above her breasts and flicked it open.

"Robert," she stammered. "We can't."

"Can't what?" Another button slipped out of its buttonhole.

"Can't, um...you know!"

"Know what?" He smiled and bent over her, pressing his lips to the pulse point at her neck and releasing another button. Then another.

His lips moved along her neck as he slid the shirt off her shoulders. His hands were gentle yet insistent as he spread the shirt on the ground and lowered her onto it.

He plucked a rose from the bush and leaned on his elbow alongside her, trailing the fragrant blossom along her skin, leaving a path of trembling desire in its wake. The petals moved over her skin like velvet, releasing a fragrant, heady aroma. Soft petals trickled onto her in a fluttering caress.

"You're so beautiful," he said, his voice husky and

tender. "An eternal, timeless beauty."

She closed her eyes, letting his voice and touch erase any lingering doubt. He brushed the velvety petals across her lips, making them throb with desire. When he grazed the blossom across her breasts she gasped, but didn't stop him. Just when she thought she couldn't stand anymore, he traced a languorous path down the center of her torso, sending ripples of pleasure through her entire body.

The sensation changed from petal-soft to rough and hot as he followed the flower's path with his lips and tongue, setting her skin on fire where he tasted her. She couldn't stop him now even if she wanted to, and she didn't ever want him to stop.

She'd never in her life relaxed and let a man make love to her like this. Slowly. Gently. Giving more than he took. She ran her fingers through his hair as he moved along her body as if she were a banquet to be savored. His unhurried, sensual movements convinced her they truly did have all the time in the world.

Every sensation intensified as she surrendered to his lovemaking. She was rocked by the rhythm of the waves lapping at the edges of the pond, caressed by the soft breeze rustling through the leaves, intoxicated by the bouquet of roses lingering in the air. A sound that was part whimper and part moan escaped her throat when his lips brushed across the sensitive skin of her thigh. She opened like a flower beneath him, a blossoming that began in her belly and spread throughout her body, extending outward in gentle waves which lifted her beyond the boundaries of time and space. There was only this moment and this man and the ecstasy she felt in his arms.

He tenderly teased her, turning her yearning into an

urgent, aching hunger, until her world became a quivering pinpoint of need and the only sound left in the universe was his name on her lips as she surrendered her body, her heart and her soul. And still he held her, easing her down so gently in a seemingly endless rhythm of warm, billowing waves.

She drifted, barely aware when he lifted her, cradling her to his chest as he carried her through the canopied forest, floating through a twilight world of verdant shadows and nimbus rays.

Gradually the cloud lifted and the world took on definition. Colors were brighter, her vision sharper. It was as if she'd been reborn. When Robert laid her gently on the bed, she felt abandoned, lost without the comfort of his arms around her, his breath, the pulsing beat of his heart. The moment it took him to undress and join her felt like an eternity.

He gathered her into his arms. "Did you miss me?"

"Desperately," she replied, welcoming him home.

He ran his hands along her back, his touch rekindling flames of desire. "You never have to," he murmured between hot, hungry kisses, his fingers moving like quicksilver along her body. "Stay with me. I've been alone so long. I never thought I'd find love again."

She wrapped her arms around him, pulling him closer. His words sparked an answering response from her own heart. It had been so long since she'd loved and been loved in return. Who knew if this chance would ever come again. She wanted to say yes, to give in to the reckless impulse and abandon everything else.

"I love you," he whispered, moving against her as if they'd made this journey through a thousand lifetimes, finding and entering her sure and smooth and filling her completely.

"Stay," he whispered urgently, taking her with a hunger matched only by her own. "Stay with me."

She arched against him, captured and enfolded him, abandoning logic for need. "Yes," she cried out, never wanting this enchanting interlude to end. "Yes, yes...yes."

CHAPTER SIXTEEN

She'd said yes in the heat of passion. Now, as the bright rays of morning struck her with blinding clarity, she wasn't so sure. If anything, Robert looked younger and more innocent in sleep, his face unlined and peaceful and softer somehow. How could she hurt him? Yet she couldn't stay without telling him the truth. There was more at stake than he knew.

His eyelids flickered and a sleepy smile curled the corners of his lips. "Hi there," he murmured.

Her heart responded quicker than her voice, fluttering in her chest when he nuzzled closer.

"Don't leave," he murmured. "You feel so good."

"I'm not going anywhere," she replied.

Yet.

He tugged her closer, fitting the hard angles of his body into her curves. She ran her fingertips across his temples and through his hair, drawing a contented sigh from him. She held him lovingly, not wanting to let him go, but knowing she had to eventually.

Yesterday seemed like a blissful dream. Or maybe her life up until now had been a dream and this was the only thing that was real—the way he held her so possessively, the sound of her name on his lips. She didn't want the dream to end, but until she could tell him everything, there would always be a distance between them that even the tightest embrace couldn't bridge.

She couldn't think with him so close, so warm and tender. Squirming out of his arms, she slipped out of bed and picked up her scattered clothes.

He stayed there, rolling onto his back and folding his arms behind his head while he watched her dress. "Aren't you going to wear my shirt?" he asked when she tucked her blouse into her pants.

"Maybe later," she said.

"Later," he repeated, smiling. "I was afraid you were going to tell me there wouldn't be a later."

She cleared her throat self-consciously. Now that he'd given her an opening and she wasn't so distracted by his touch, she tried to find a way let him down gently. "Robert. I have a job and responsibilities back in New York. I can't stay here."

He stared into her eyes and she looked away. Finally, breaking the silence, he said, "We can discuss that. If it's a problem, I'll move to New York with you."

Her eyes widened. "But your cottage—"

He shrugged. "We'll find a new place to live. I'll build you a cottage we can fill with our own memories."

Liz turned so he wouldn't see the emotions on her face. It was one thing to entertain the thought of staying here with him, surrounded by the magic that put them on an equal footing—but to bring him back to her world? She couldn't even begin to tell him the problems that would cause. Plus it would mean allowing him to see her the way she really was. Oh, maybe she could have a little nip and tuck—peeling, lifting, liposuction—but there was no way medical science could compete with magic. She'd never again look the way she did when she was his age—the way she did here in the cottage.

"Robert," she said. "I'm older than I look."

To her surprise he laughed, a hearty chuckle that shook the bed. "So am I," he said. "I considered growing a beard to make myself look my age, but it itches."

He wasn't taking her seriously. Why should he? How could she explain one thing when his eyes told him another.

She sighed, stepping into her shoes. "I'm serious."

"So am I," he said, the smile disappearing from his face. "Do you think I care about age? Do you think I'm that shallow? Nothing matters but the way we feel about each other." He sat up and held out his hand. "Come here."

She walked back across the room, taking his outstretched hand. He cradled it gently, then brought it to his cheek and tipped his face against her open palm, holding it there.

"I love you," he said. "Nothing else matters." He turned his face and kissed the center of her palm. "Whatever worries or concerns you have, we can talk about them. We'll work them out."

She wished it were that simple. He made it sound as if their love could overcome anything. She didn't argue, letting his gentle assurances work their magic on her, convincing her they could find a way around the barriers she foresaw.

"We have a lot to talk about," he said. "But we have all the time in the world. I want to know everything there is to know about you—your life, your dreams *and* your worries. I promise you that whatever it is you're so afraid of, there's no need to be. I love you." He kissed each of her fingers in turn, repeating the statement with each kiss. "I love you. I love you and you deserve that. *We* deserve it."

She couldn't argue with his conviction. She did deserve some happiness. She'd always sacrificed for everyone around her at her own expense. Now she had no one who needed her, no obligations other than her own. Why couldn't she reach out and take what he offered?

"I'll go get my things," she whispered.

He squeezed her hand a moment before releasing it. "You'll be back, right?"

"Yes," she assured him. "I'll be back as soon as I've checked out of the bed and breakfast. Then we'll talk and take it from there."

He gave an immense sigh of relief and let her go. "I'll be waiting," he said. "For as long as it takes."

She knew he would, but it wouldn't take her long. She only had a few things to pack before paying her bill and checking out. She'd be back in his arms before he'd had a chance to miss her.

*　*　*

Back at Stone Haven, Liz rushed up the stairs toward her room. She was at the top when Amanda called up to her. "Ms. Riley? I meant to tell you—"

Liz kept going, in a hurry to get her things and get back to Robert as soon as she could. "I'll be right back down," she called, cutting the woman off and turning the corner.

She swung open the door and froze, her jaw dropping when she saw the man pacing the small room. He stopped and stared at her accusingly.

"Teddy?"

"Where were you all night?" her son demanded.

"I..." She shook her head. What was he doing here?

He looked awful, as if he'd been pacing for hours, running his hands through his hair the way he always did when he was upset.

"Don't say you were here," he said, "because I've been here all night waiting for you. Where have you been?"

She didn't like the sound of his voice or the way his accusations made her feel. "I stayed the night with a friend," she said, trying to brush the wrinkles from her clothes.

He cocked an eyebrow at her accusingly. "A friend?" he snorted. "I've heard rumors about a so-called friend, but I figured it was small-town gossip."

She didn't respond to that. He had no right to give her the third degree. She considered telling him she'd been with a man young enough to be his brother, but this wasn't the way to break it to him. Not now when he was so angry. She straightened her shoulders, avoiding the subject. "What are you doing here?" she asked.

"As if..." he started, then bit back the comment Liz knew would have hurt them both. "Marcie's sick," he said, his shoulders slumping. "She needs you."

"Oh my God!" Her anger over Teddy's patronizing attitude vanished. She ran to him and put her arms around him. "What's wrong? How sick is she?"

He crumbled, becoming a scared little boy again the moment she held him. She knew his anger was more from fear than anything else.

"Real sick, Mom. That's why I came to get you. I'll tell you on the way." He glanced at his watch. "There's a flight leaving in about an hour. Can you be ready in time?"

"I'm ready right now," she said, throwing her

suitcase open and packing the few things she'd left around the room while he called to confirm their seats. She zippered the suitcase and reached for her keys, realizing she'd have to make arrangements for her car while she was gone.

She turned to Teddy. "I have a loaner from the garage. It'll only take a minute to drop it off and make arrangements to have them store my car until I can get it back."

He glanced at his watch again and nodded. While she checked out of the Bed and Breakfast, he loaded her luggage into his rental car, then followed her to the garage.

She'd hoped for a few moments to explain to Herb, but Teddy followed her into the office. It was bad enough that she couldn't call Robert and explain personally with Teddy there. Now she couldn't even explain fully to Herb so he could pass the message on for her.

"I have a family emergency," she told Herb. "I have to fly to California. Could you store my car here until I can get back?"

"Of course," Herb said, glancing suspiciously over her shoulder at Teddy. "Is everything all right?"

"Yes," she assured him. "But I don't know how long I'll be gone." She lowered her voice. "Would you tell Robert? Please? Tell him I'll be back."

Herb squeezed her hand and nodded. "Of course. Don't worry," he said, raising his voice for Teddy's benefit. "Your car will be fine here until you get back."

"How much are you going to charge to store the car?" Teddy asked gruffly.

"No charge," Herb said to Liz, ignoring Teddy. "Just take care of yourself and don't worry about a thing."

Liz nodded gratefully as her son bustled her out the door.

* * *

Robert kept himself busy. He imagined Tallulah's quiet air of watchfulness from the corner signaled her approval. First he made room in his closet for Liz's clothes and emptied two full dresser drawers for her to use. She'd need more space later, but this should be enough for whatever she had with her right now.

With the necessities taken care of, he turned to the niceties. He decorated the bedroom with flowers—mixed bouquets of cut wildflowers with an arrangement of long-stemmed red roses beside the bed. He placed candles around the room and sprinkled a handful of rose petals over the bed. Satisfied that everything was perfect, he closed the door and went to the kitchen.

"Now," he said aloud. "What shall I make for dinner?"

Tallulah didn't seem to have an opinion one way or the other, so Robert scoured the contents of the refrigerator himself for ingredients. He wanted dinner to be perfect—their first meal on the first day of their life together.

It would be, too. Once he had a chance to explain everything, she'd realize how groundless her fears were. He'd prove to her once and for all that they were meant for each other. Before the evening was over, she'd believe in destiny. She'd believe in him.

* * *

Liz slumped into her seat. They'd barely made it in

time and only Teddy's high-decibel insistence that they were on their way to her daughter's deathbed convinced the attendant to allow them onto the plane, which was already boarded and awaiting take-off.

She tried to fasten her seatbelt, but her hands shook and she couldn't seem to get the pieces to connect. The word *deathbed* echoed over and over in her mind. While she'd been selfishly enjoying herself, her daughter had been dying. Now she might not get there in time. She deserved whatever recriminations her son threw at her.

Teddy reached over and fastened the seatbelt for her. He took her trembling hand and leaned over, whispering so only she could hear. "Calm down. It's not as bad as I made out to the attendant. There isn't another flight until tomorrow and I promised Marcie I'd have you there today, no matter what, so I exaggerated a little."

"She's not dying?"

"No," he admitted. "But she's in the hospital and she needs you."

Liz didn't know whether to smack him for nearly giving her a stroke or hold him tight. The thought of losing one of her children was too much to bear.

"Tell me exactly what's wrong."

"Well," he said. "She's been run down since the baby was born. After you left, she developed a cough, but she figured it was just a cold and didn't bother seeing a doctor. Yesterday she couldn't breathe and was too weak to get out of bed. Dan rushed her to the emergency room. It might be pneumonia. They don't know for sure yet."

Silent tears ran from her eyes. She couldn't shake the guilt that assaulted her. She was besieged with *should have's*. I should have stayed with her longer. I should have known something was wrong when she called, but I was too anxious to get back to my own selfish tryst. I should have been there when she needed me, not acting irresponsibly like someone half my age.

Teddy squeezed her hand. "She's gonna be fine, Mom. She just needs you there."

Liz nodded numbly. She leaned her forehead against the cool glass of the window, watching the miles slip away. The words she'd said to Herb echoed with a hollow emptiness through her mind. "Tell him I'll be back." The words haunted her as the Rocky Mountains faded from sight.

Slowly the pull of enchantment released her as worry and guilt replaced her tentative belief in magic.

CHAPTER SEVENTEEN

Robert watched the stars climb in the midnight sky. Flickering pinpoints of light deepened the inky blackness of the night, making him feel small and even more alone. He wondered if somewhere Liz was looking at the same sky, counting the same stars. She'd been gone for two days and he hadn't heard a word from her. He was starting to wonder if he ever would.

He closed the door on the night and went inside. The flowers he'd placed around the room had long-since wilted, the candles remained unlit. He hadn't slept in his own bed since Liz left. It felt too big for one.

When the phone rang he nearly tripped over himself to answer it. It was only Herb. Robert fought the urge to have Herb go over every detail of that morning all over again. Had Liz looked afraid? Was there any clue who the man with her was? Did she say what kind of family emergency? Are you sure she didn't leave a forwarding number?

He'd already asked all those questions enough times to try the patience of a saint. Asking them again wouldn't change the answers. Herb didn't know any more than he'd already said.

Robert fielded Herb's request to come over for dinner. Even the offer of Janie's fresh-baked banana bread couldn't sway him. He had no appetite for either food or small talk.

He paced around the cottage, too restless to settle in one place. The things that normally would have given him enjoyment—a roaring fire, music and a good book—held no appeal. There was only one thing he wanted and she'd disappeared.

He felt helpless and frustrated not being able to do anything. He'd called Amanda at Stone Haven, but that had been a dead end. She didn't know where Liz went or who the man was who'd come to get her. Liz had paid the bill by check and Amanda had been more than willing to give Robert the phone number and address from her records. He'd tried the number in New York, but there'd been no answer. Still, he called every hour or so just to hear her voice on the answering machine.

He rubbed his hand over the rough bristle of his jaw. Even the scratchy rawness of stubble was better than feeling nothing at all. He probably looked like hell, but shaving was too much of an effort and there didn't seem to be much point to it anyway. Tallulah certainly didn't care what he looked like.

He couldn't stop wondering about the man Herb had seen with Liz. Who was he? He must be a relative. She'd said it was a family emergency, but that didn't stop him from feeling a dark cloud of jealousy. What if he was something more?

His pacing eventually took him to the room Liz had used the first night she'd stayed at the cottage. He wished she'd left something behind. Something he could touch that belonged to her. Something he could remember her by. She'd taken her slippers when she left. There was nothing he could hold in his hand that still carried her imprint.

Then he saw it. Shoved to the back corner of the dresser where she'd left it that first night. Her travel alarm clock. He remembered stopping her when she'd attempted to wind it. He should have told her then. Now it might be too late.

Robert held the clock in his hands. Finally there was something he could do. One thing he had control of.

He took a deep breath and began winding the clock, feeling the gears grinding and tightening. When the key stopped turning, he set it on the dresser. A sense of destiny filled the room, the air thick with the passage of time. The ticking of the clock was the only sound in the cottage. He reached into his pocket for the ring Liz had found beside the gazebo, reading the inscription to himself, then placing it beside the ticking clock.

* * *

Liz remembered a quote from The Glass Menagerie. *"For time is the longest distance between two points."* Tennessee Williams could have been writing about her. She wondered whether she and Robert could ever bridge the gap of time.

The house was quiet. Marcie and the baby were both napping, Dan was at work, and Teddy had returned home a few days ago. By the time she'd arrived from Colorado, Marcie had already been released from the hospital with a diagnosis of bronchitis rather than pneumonia. Liz had thrown herself into caring for her daughter and the household, trying not to think of what she'd left behind.

After a week of total bed rest and antibiotics, Marcie was nearly back on her feet, but still Liz coddled her, taking care of the house and the baby while Marcie got her strength back. She'd be good as new soon, but Liz wasn't ready to leave. She still hadn't decided what she'd do when it was time to go.

It had only been a week since she'd left the magic of the cottage behind, but it seemed more like a lifetime. At first she'd been so worried about Marcie and so busy taking care of the baby that she hadn't had much time to think about Robert.

Now that the danger was over, memories came flooding back. Their brief interlude together had taken on a dreamlike quality and she sometimes wondered whether she'd invented the whole thing. Every morning when she looked at herself in the mirror she suspected Teddy was right and she was simply going through a mid-life crisis.

Then Robert's face would come to mind and make her smile, or she'd hear a song that reminded her of him and get lost in a daydream. She'd promised him she'd return and she knew he was waiting for her to keep that promise. She puttered around the bright, lemon-yellow kitchen, feeling a thousand miles away from the green mountains of Colorado.

The front door opened and Marcie's husband, Dan, came in from work, a bouquet of red roses in his hand. Liz smiled. He was a good man—loving and caring. If she could have hand picked a husband for her daughter, she would have chosen him.

He walked in and kissed her on the cheek. "Something smells good," he said, sniffing the air.

"Roast beef," Liz replied.

He cocked his head. "How's everyone doing today?"

"Wonderful. They're both sleeping. Marcie's starting to get a little restless, which is a good sign." She reached in the upper cabinet for a vase and took the roses from his hands. "She'll love these."

Dan shook his head. "They're not for Marcie. They're for you." He gave her a warm hug. "You've been an angel and I don't know how we would have gotten by without your help."

She was touched. "Oh, Dan. Thank you." At the same time she wondered if it might not be her cue that as much as they appreciated her help, it was time for them to pull together as a family now.

With a trembling hand, Liz reached out and touched the petals of the rose, remembering the way Robert had traced rose petals along her skin beside the gazebo. A shiver rippled down her spine as she was assaulted by memories of his soft voice, his velvety touch. She knew she had to go back. She just didn't know what she'd tell Robert when she got there.

With a brisk wave, Liz shooed Dan off to be with Marcie while she set the table, bustling around the kitchen and getting everything ready for dinner. While it felt good to be needed, this was only temporary. She could hear their voices whispering in the other room. It would be good for them to be alone together once again.

Soon they joined her, Marcie leaning on Dan's arm, weak but smiling.

"How are you feeling, honey?" Liz asked.

Marcie settled herself carefully into a chair while Dan prepared a cup of tea at the kitchen counter. "I'm feeling so much better," she said.

"You look good," Liz said, sitting across from her and taking her hand. It was cooler. The fever had broken yesterday and Marcie even had some color to her cheeks now.

"So do you, Mom. I've been meaning to ask you what you've done to yourself. You look wonderful."

Liz cocked her head. "How so?"

"I don't know. There's something about you. You look younger. Happier. I haven't seen you look this way since Dad died."

The thought brought Liz up short. Younger? It was too easy to believe that she'd been fooling herself all along. Maybe there wasn't any magic in the cottage after all. Maybe it was love that had made her feel so young and alive.

Dan placed the cup of tea in front of Marcie, brushing his fingers lovingly through her hair before going into the living room and leaving them alone to talk. He turned on the radio and as if on cue, Liz heard the familiar strains of *Stardust* playing softly in the background. The memory of Robert's voice caught her off guard.

Do you believe in magic? Do you believe in destiny?

She closed her eyes, letting the music carry her back to Colorado and an enchanted cottage where time stood still. So he was younger. Did it really matter? When he'd asked that same question, it had. Now she wasn't so sure.

"Mom?" Marcie had a puzzled smile on her face.

Liz looked up. "Hmm?"

"If I didn't know better I'd say you looked like a woman in love."

Liz squeezed her hand, but didn't deny it. "What would you say if I told you I was?"

Marcie's eyes widened. "What? What are you saying?"

"I've fallen hopelessly, desperately, head-over-heels in love with a man I met in Colorado." There, it was out, and Marcie didn't look shocked or surprised.

Marcie cocked her head, staring as if seeing her mother in a new light. Then she smiled and wrapped her arms around her mother's shoulders. "Mom! That's wonderful."

Liz let out a sigh of relief. She'd expected shock and disapproval from her children, afraid they'd think she was being disloyal to Ted's memory. However, Marcie's enthusiasm seemed genuine.

"We just want you to be happy, Mom. You've been alone too long."

So Liz told Marcie as much as she could, surprising herself with how much she knew about Robert and how real he became in the telling.

When she was done, Marcie asked her what she was still doing here and not back in Colorado with him.

"There are some problems," Liz explained. "He's...well, he's a bit younger than I am. I was afraid of what people would think."

"Does he make you happy?"

"Yes. He makes me deliriously happy."

"Does he love you as much as you love him?"

"If that's possible, yes he does."

Marcie sat up straight. "Then there doesn't seem to be anything to worry about, does there?"

As pleased as she was with Marcie's acceptance, Liz knew Teddy wouldn't be as easy to win over. "Your brother seems to think I'm having a mid-life crisis," she said.

"Mom, you're young and vibrant and a beautiful woman. You deserve to be happy. Teddy's a grown man with a life of his own. He may or may not approve, but he *will* understand. Teddy loves you and wants you to be happy, just like I do."

Liz suddenly felt light and free, no longer weighed down by worries and guilt. Marcie was right. She didn't need her children's permission any more than they needed hers for the choices they made. She had a right to be happy. Life was too short to waste a single moment.

"Go to him, Mom," Marcie said, echoing her own conviction.

She would, but she would go on her own terms, without hiding behind a cloak of magic. If he really loved her, it wouldn't matter how old she was.

She was surprised to realize that it no longer mattered to her, either. She didn't need the enchantment of the cottage. She didn't need to be young again. It wasn't really her youth she missed, but the loss of her dreams. She'd become jaded by everyday routine; allowed herself to grow old because she'd turned her back on life and love and adventure. Would she give up this chance to regain it without a fight? Did it matter what anyone else thought?

No.

She loved Robert and he loved her, and that was the only thing that mattered.

That night, packing for her trip back to Colorado, Liz took a cold, hard look at herself in the mirror. So, she wasn't twenty-five. Or thirty. But would she want to be again?

She was proud of what the stretch marks on her skin represented, and the years had given her an understanding of life that no twenty-year old could even grasp. It had to be lived to be understood. The trade-off was a few fine lines, crackling joints, a bit of sag, a touch of silver, and extra pigmentation here and there— roadmarks on the path of life.

She smiled at her reflection and there was a beauty that radiated outward from her eyes. If Robert was the man she thought he was, that was the beauty that would matter to him—not the physical proof of time's passage.

But she had to be sure.

CHAPTER EIGHTEEN

Liz gazed dreamily out the airplane window. She was going home. Not to New York. Not to her empty bungalow on Elm Street or her sterile nurse's cubicle at Pleasant Valley Elementary. She was going to Coldwater Springs, Colorado—a place she'd never heard of a month ago, but which felt more like home than any other place on earth.

The seat beside her was empty. She'd hoped to be alone for the trip so she could think about the changes she was contemplating in her life, but a young woman had boarded late and taken the aisle seat. They'd nodded to each other politely, then Liz had put her headphones on and the girl had opened a book on her lap. The empty seat between them afforded a small cushion of privacy, for which Liz was grateful. She wasn't in the mood for small talk.

She seemed to be floating on a blanket of clouds, in more ways than one. Beneath her the earth glimmered like a jewel through openings in the cloud cover. She slipped the headphones off. The music only distracted her from her thoughts of a cottage nestled in the mountainside and the man waiting for her there. She wondered if he could feel her thoughts reaching out to him, if he knew she was coming home.

She settled back in the seat and sighed, running her

fingers through her hair. There was still a bit of a lump on the side of her head from when the car had spun out of control. It seemed like an eternity ago. What strange twist of destiny had brought her to Robert's doorstep? An unmarked back road, a sudden storm, her car breaking down just beyond his cottage, the electrical failure that kept her there instead of being able to get outside help. It made one believe in destiny after all. Or...

She traced the outline of the lump again. A head injury, hallucinations, wishful thinking, a figment of her imagination. Would Robert really be there when she arrived? What if she couldn't find the road again? What if the mysterious cottage had disappeared, carried off on the wings of the same enchantment that had placed it in her path? What if she'd turned her back on her one wish and the genie had snatched it all away and flown back into the bottle? Would she ever get another chance?

Then just as quickly the doubts struck again. What am I doing? She'd never been an impulsive person, yet here she was prepared to turn her back on everything for a man she'd only known a few weeks. It meant changing her whole self image. She'd always been predictable, stable, level-headed. Like Robert had said, she always colored within the lines, doing what was right and expected of her.

Until now. There was still time to reconsider, however. She could stay on the plane and continue on to her real life instead of embracing a fantasy. That's what it was, really. A fantasy. A dream.

Suddenly, without warning, the plane pitched then dropped straight down, losing altitude with a mind-numbing speed. For a moment she was weightless, pulled against the straining seat belt as they fell, fell, fell for a soundless eternity. She gripped the armrests and drew in a quick, sharp breath as her stomach clenched and churned. Then she grew quiet all over. No fear or dread, just a strangely calm sense of inevitability. She felt as if she was floating, every sense alert and watching in ice-cold fascination.

"My God, my God, my God," she murmured.

Then a hand closed around hers, squeezing tight and breaking through the shock. She squeezed back. Squeezed with all her strength, grateful for that moment of human contact, the touch of another person. Just then the plane jerked, like a yo-yo pulled up at the end of its string.

They were moving again. They weren't crashing. Liz let out a long, trembling sigh of relief.

"Air pocket," the woman beside her said.

"Yes." Liz looked gratefully into the woman's eyes, unable to release the clenched hand just yet. "Air pocket."

"It's all right. Everything's all right." The woman smiled and there seemed to be more understanding in the compassionate depths of her eyes than her words implied. Suddenly the plane was alive with sounds, relieved voices chattered, as if everyone had been torn loose from the same grip of terror.

The pilot's announcement over the loudspeaker confirmed the situation and informed the passengers they were regaining altitude. With an embarrassed laugh, Liz released her death grip on the woman's hand. "Thank you," she said.

"Scary, isn't it?"

Liz nodded, still not trusting her voice.

"Makes you think." There seemed to be an ancient

wisdom in those eyes. Her voice was calmly measured. "Life is so short. We never know, do we? I suppose all we can do is live our life to the fullest and, when the time comes, leave without regrets."

Her words touched a chord in Liz. No matter what other concerns she had, that was the ultimate truth. Life was too short to let doubts and rules and insecurities rob you of whatever happiness it had to offer. Life was too short and love too precious to deny.

"Yes," she whispered. Then stronger, a smile punctuating the affirmation. "Yes."

"Where are you going?" her companion asked.

Without a thread of doubt, Liz replied, "To Coldwater Springs, Colorado. To be with the man I love."

The woman nodded with approval, as if that was exactly the answer she'd been expecting. "Well, good luck. He must be a lucky man."

"No," Liz replied. "I'm the lucky one."

The woman chuckled, the sound clear and sweet, like water rippling over the shore. "Love's funny like that." She reached around for her buckle and unfastened it. "I want to check on a friend in the back of the plane. Will you be all right?"

"Yes," Liz replied. There was no question in her mind. She'd be all right from here on in.

As the woman turned and started to walk away, Liz called out. "Wait! I didn't get your name." For some reason it was important to know the name of the woman who'd held her hand and comforted her at the moment of greatest fear.

The woman's eyes twinkled and an enigmatic smile crossed her face. "Hope," she replied. "My name is

Hope."

As clearly as if he were standing beside her, she heard Robert's voice. "*Hope. It's more than just a name. It's a choice.*"

Liz's breath caught in her throat. The moment stretched between them, filled with a sense of destiny. "Hope," she repeated, and it sounded like a prayer. "Thank you, Hope."

The woman nodded and smiled, then turned away.

* * *

In an enchanted cottage far below, a red rose, perfectly preserved in timeless beauty, lay nestled between a ticking clock and a shimmering band of gold. Robert waited, listening to the measured beat of time passing.

"I understand what you were asking, now" he said aloud. The scent of roses surrounded him and he smiled. "I'll always love you, Elise, but I realize it's time to move on. Time to love again."

As if in answer, the curtains fluttered briefly, then fell still.

CHAPTER NINETEEN

Liz never saw Hope again, although she'd searched the lines of departing passengers and the bustling crowd in the airport terminal. Somehow it didn't surprise her. She was a believer now. She believed in destiny, she believed in love, she believed in magic.

There was just one little problem left. She had to let Robert see her the way she really was. She had to face him outside the radius of enchantment. And she had to hope it didn't change anything. Her first impulse was to run right to the cottage and enjoy one last glorious moment of youth in his arms. That would be cheating, though, and would only make the moment of truth that much harder to face.

So instead she took her old room at the bed and breakfast, where she tried to work up the courage to call Robert. Twice she'd dialed. The first time she'd punched three numbers before hanging up. The second time she'd gotten all the way to five. Each time she'd chickened out.

Maybe a letter would be easier. She could explain everything and tell him why she didn't break the illusion before now. She could tell him about her children, her fear that he wouldn't love a woman her age. She could tell him about the woman on the plane and how she finally believed in destiny and magic. God, she had so much to tell him! If only she could finish dialing the phone.

Before she could try again, there was a knock on the door. Could Robert have found her already? She wasn't ready to face him yet. What would she say? The second knock was louder, more insistent.

"Coming," she called, running her fingers quickly through her hair. There wasn't time for more than that. She tried to prepare herself as she opened the door.

But it wasn't Robert. "Amanda told me you were back," Janie said, bustling into the room.

Liz let out a sigh of relief, feeling as if she'd dodged a bullet. There was still time to prepare herself for the confrontation ahead. "I just got in," she said, closing the door. She gestured to her still packed luggage beside the bed.

Janie nodded. "I mainly came to tell you that your car's ready. Robert's frantic. He calls every day to see if we've heard from you. Plus, well...I've missed you."

"Oh Janie." Liz reached out and hugged the woman who in such a short time had become both a friend and confidant. "I missed you, too."

"I was so worried. Herb said it was a family emergency. Is everything all right?"

Liz explained her daughter's illness and assured Janie that everything was fine. "She's ready to get on with her own life now."

"And you? Are you ready to get on with your own life?"

Liz nodded. "More than you know."

Janie chewed on her lower lip. "We were afraid you wouldn't come back."

Liz didn't reply. There had been times she wasn't sure she would, either. She couldn't promise Janie she was back for good, though. Not yet. It all depended on Robert and his reaction to her.

"You said Robert called every day?" she asked.

Janie sighed. "Sometimes twice a day. He drove Herb crazy with questions. '*Did she say where she was going? What kind of family emergency? Did she look frightened? How did the man with her act?*' I think he was afraid you were being kidnapped by a crazed serial killer."

Liz chuckled. "That man was my son. He's crazed, but hasn't killed anyone as far as I know." She was still mad at Teddy for scaring her half to death, but when she'd called to explain why she was returning to Colorado, she was surprised to find the conversation wasn't as hard as she'd expected. While his enthusiasm hadn't been as immediate as Marcie's, he'd eventually come around.

Liz cleared her throat nervously. "Janie, Robert doesn't know I have grown children."

"Why would that bother him?"

Liz shrugged. "I don't know." She realized Janie had no knowledge of the cottage's temporary effect on her, but surely she must realize that the difference in their ages would be a problem.

"Liz, I have to be honest with you. I was so upset when you left. Not only for myself, but for Robert. I haven't seen him this happy in so long. I thought he'd remain closed off and shuttered away forever. It was as if he'd been in a deep, deep sleep. Then you came along and awakened something in him."

Liz smiled at the image. Like Elise's treasured *Sleeping Beauty*, only this time it was the prince awakened by a kiss.

"You know," Janie continued. "I haven't known you

168

for that long, but I would suspect he's done the same for you. Am I right?"

Liz nodded. "Yes, but there are other things to be worked out."

"Then call him. Work them out."

"I will," Liz replied with a grateful smile.

Janie turned before opening the door. "If for some reason you can't work things out, please don't leave without saying goodbye."

Liz hugged her. "I won't. I promise."

When Janie left, the room was quiet with expectation. This time Liz managed to dial all the way through to the end and Robert answered on the first ring.

"Robert? It's Liz." Her voice trembled. "I'm back."

There was a pause at the other end of the line. "No," he said. "You're not back yet. You won't really be back until you're here in my arms."

"Oh, Robert." The telephone amplified the satin-smooth texture of his voice, and the sweetness of his words made her knees weak.

"Come home, Liz. Come back to the cottage."

At that moment she wanted nothing more than to slip away into the enchantment of his embrace, but she knew she had to be strong—even if it meant breaking the spell irrevocably.

"We have so much to talk about first," she said. "There are things I need to tell you."

"We'll talk. We'll talk all night, all week. We'll do nothing but talk for the rest of our lives if that's what you want."

"Robert, there are things you don't know about me."

"I know all I need to know."

"I'm older. I have kids."

"It doesn't matter. There are things you don't know about me, too. All you need to know right now is that I love you. Nothing else matters."

"But..."

"Say it, Liz. Say it doesn't matter."

"It doesn't..." She faltered.

"Go on, say it."

He waited in silence while she tried to form the words. He seemed prepared to wait forever. She closed her eyes and took a deep breath, making the commitment he waited for. "It doesn't matter. Only love matters."

Liz desperately wanted to believe that, but it wasn't enough to simply say the words. She'd know the truth when she saw it in his eyes.

She heard him let out a breath, as if he'd been holding it waiting for her response.

"Robert," she whispered. "Could you meet me here in town? It's important to me."

"I'll meet you wherever you want," he replied. "Just say when."

"An hour?"

"I'll be there," he promised.

She spent the time preparing, taking extra care with her make-up and hair. Marcie was right. She looked better than she had in years. There was a glow to her skin, a sparkle in her eyes, and a spring to her step that had nothing to do with magic. Unless it was the magic of love.

She didn't look twenty, but she looked lovely nonetheless. She looked her age, and she could be objective about that now that she wasn't seeing herself reflected through eyes that had lost hope. Surely Robert would see the woman behind those eyes was the same one he fell in love with. If not, he wasn't the man she thought he was.

That didn't stop her from trembling, however. Everything hinged on his reaction. Not only today, but tomorrow and the day after. Maybe he was ready to disregard the difference in their ages right now, but what about ten years from now? Twenty? The gulf would widen as the years progressed.

Everyone knew that men aged better than women. He had years of youthful vitality left, while she'd already begun her decline, a decline that would pick up speed like the final plunge of a four-star roller coaster ride. In ten years he'd only look better, while she her shine began to dim. And then what? Neck wattles ran in her family. Eventually the day would come when they walked into a restaurant and the waiter asked what the gentleman and his mother would like.

"You're just looking for problems, aren't you?" she chided herself. The urge to run again was strong. She wasn't sure she could bear it if disappointment clouded his eyes.

The knock came sooner than she expected. Where had the time gone? She checked her watch, surprised to see that an hour had gone by in what had felt like only minutes. Time was funny like that, stretching and compressing to suit its own whims. Where before it had raced with the speed of a whirlwind, it now seemed to stand still. She could count every beat of her heart, feel every breath expand and contract in her lungs.

"Liz? It's Robert." His voice was muffled from the other side of the door.

She couldn't move. The door seemed a thousand miles away across the room. She tried to call out, but her voice was a thin squeak. Slowly, as if slogging through oatmeal, she made her way to the door.

Her hand shook as she reached for the doorknob, closing around the cool brass. Then turning. Slowly, slowly she opened the door, stepping back as the slivered opening widened. She had to remind herself it was Robert on the other side. The man she'd grown to know and love and trust.

She swung the door open, then stopped, her eyes widening in surprise. Robert stared back at her, but it was a Robert she'd never seen before. He was still the same man, but different. Older. Just as she was.

Liz studied the familiar face, now chiseled with character lines. A new beard—streaked with white to match the salt and pepper of his hair—softened the sharp angles of his jaw. Beneath the signs of age, she could still see the man she loved. Those same blue eyes twinkled from the face now marked by the passage of time, and the same gentle humor curled the corners of this lips.

With a joyous cry, Liz threw herself into his waiting arms, burying her face against the side of his neck. Robert, her Robert! His arms tightened around her, holding her close as the last barrier between them melted away.

Suddenly it all fell into place. The magic of the cottage hadn't affected only her, but him too. It affected anyone who crossed the boundary. No wonder he hadn't let anyone inside the cottage. If he hadn't been forced to let her in, she'd have never seen him as young, either.

That also explained why Janie hadn't seemed surprised at all by the age difference. Beyond the cottage walls, she'd seen Robert age gradually along with the rest of them.

"So," he asked, releasing her for a moment and stepping back to look into her eyes. "Does it matter?"

He seemed to be holding his breath waiting for her answer. "No," she said, feeling a smile she couldn't contain break out on her face. She reached up and stroked his cheek, loving him more than she thought possible. "You were right. Age doesn't matter at all."

EPILOGUE

Liz was packing when Robert came in. He leaned against the doorway watching her, his hand behind his back. She glanced up and smiled. "What do you have there?"

He sauntered toward her, holding out a perfect red rose. "A timeless beauty. Just like you."

She blushed. Even without magic, he made her feel young and carefree and alive. But most of all he made her feel treasured. Adored. She loved him more than words could say.

She lowered her eyes. "Do you still think I'm beautiful?"

He met her gaze. "More beautiful now than the day I met you."

"You always say exactly the right thing." Like twin souls, she thought. He knows the secret, hidden parts of me.

She looked around the cottage. It was still magical. It always would be. Robert had explained that the spell had been broken when he wound the clock she'd left behind, setting time in motion again. Whether it was the physical action of winding the clock or his decision to move forward with his life wasn't important. Robert insisted her love had broken the spell which had kept him locked in time.

Whatever it was, the spell had been broken. They'd remained unchanged when they'd returned to the cottage. So had Janie and Herb when they'd invited them over to celebrate their engagement.

As if reading her thoughts, Robert asked. "Do you miss it? Do you miss being young?"

"No," she said, wrapping her arms around him. "You make me young. Your love is the only magic I'll ever need."

"Good answer," he said, tucking the rose behind her ear and brushing his fingers along her cheek.

As the weeks had passed, Liz had almost convinced herself that the cottage's enchantment had all been an illusion. Beauty is in the eyes of the beholder, and they'd seen each other through eyes clouded with love.

"I'll miss the cottage," she said, closing the suitcase.

"We'll be back," he assured her. "And Janie and Herb have agreed to be caretakers until we return."

"I'll miss them, too."

"Oh, honey." He held her close. "It won't be long. And they promised to come to the wedding."

She smiled. They'd already exchanged their own private vows beneath the gazebo with Tallulah as their witness, but there'd be a formal Christmas wedding with everyone they loved in attendance. Herb and Janie had promised to fly out to New York and Liz had sworn there'd been tears in Herb's eyes when Robert had asked him to be his best man.

Robert brushed his lips across her forehead. "So," he asked, "do you think your kids will like me?"

She looked up and held his gaze. "They'll love you. How can they not love you as much as I do?"

He took a deep breath, holding her close. "I'd

resigned myself to living the rest of my life alone in this cottage, with only memories to keep me company. I never dared hope I could be this happy."

He placed a finger beneath her chin and tipped her face to his, kissing her with a tenderness that tugged at her heart.

"Listen," he said, tilting his head. "They're playing our song."

She heard the opening strains of *Stardust* drifting from the radio. It didn't surprise her. There was still a little magic left in the cottage. She let him lead her in a slow dance, knowing she'd found her destiny right here in his arms.

* * *

That night Liz dreamed again. In the dream, she made her way through misty forests to the gazebo where a slim, leather-bound book beckoned her. She sat on the step and lifted the book to her lap with a sense of calm. Somehow she knew that this time she'd be able to make out the words. Moonlight rippled along the surface of the supple leather. As she flipped open the page, the words blurred, then took on substance. She ran her finger over the magical phrase, knowing it was the final message she would receive from Elise.

Her lips moved as she mouthed the words. *"And they lived happily ever after."*

THE END

About the Author

Linda began her writing career publishing short fiction for women's magazines. Since then, she's completed several award-winning novels in a variety of genres, from rib-tickling comedy to bone-chilling suspense. Reviewers have hailed her work as unique, original, and impossible to put down.

Linda is the proud recipient of the EPPIE Award, the Dream Realm Award, the Dorothy Parker Reviewers Choice Award, and several readers' choice awards. A transplanted New Yorker, Linda and her husband have retired to sunny Florida where she continues to write on the beach or poolside.

Other Books by this Author

House of Cry
Glory Girls
Tales Told by Moonlight
Heaven and Lace
The Chance You Take
East of Easy
Soul Shards
The King's Gold